By Will Weaver

*Snares* (1982)
*Striking Out* (1993)
*Farm Team* (1995)
*Hard Ball* (1998)
*Memory Boy* (2001)
*Claws* (2003)
*Full Service* (2005)
*Defect* (2007)

For Adults

*Red Earth, White Earth* (1987)
*A Gravestone Made of Wheat
and Other Stories* (1990)
*Sweet Land: New and Selected Stories* (2006)

# DEFECT

# WILL WEAVER

# DEFECT

FARRAR, STRAUS AND GIROUX
NEW YORK

Copyright © 2007 by Will Weaver
All rights reserved
Distributed in Canada by Douglas & McIntyre Ltd.
Printed in the United States of America
Designed by Jay Colvin
First edition, 2007
1   3   5   7   9   10   8   6   4   2

www.fsgkidsbooks.com

Library of Congress Cataloging-in-Publication Data
Weaver, Will.
    Defect / Will Weaver.— 1st ed.
        p.   cm.
    Summary: After spending most of his life in Minnesota foster homes
hiding a bizarre physical abnormality, fifteen-year-old David is offered a
chance at normalcy, but must decide if giving up what makes him special
is the right thing to do.
    ISBN-13: 978-0-374-31725-6
    ISBN-10: 0-374-31725-9
    [1. Abnormalities, Human—Fiction.   2. Foster home care—Fiction.
3. Self-acceptance—Fiction.   4. High schools—Fiction.   5. Schools—
Fiction.   6. Farm life—Minnesota—Fiction.   7. Minnesota—Fiction.]
I. Title.

PZ7.W3623 Def 2007
[Fic]—dc22

                                                              2006049152

*To all young readers
who know hospitals too well*

# DEFECT

|

The fight is going down tonight. By the time school lets
out, word has spread. Even the Student Council types
who have thrown the rare "Hey" David's way turn their
backs on him.

"Just because you look weird, that's no reason why you
have to *act* weird," kids whisper.

"If people like David just tried to fit in, they wouldn't
have so much trouble."

"It's really not Kael's fault."

That would be Kael Grimes, David's main tormentor.
David's ingrown hair. David's zit that never goes away.
This is Minnesota, where people stare at anything new
or different, but Kael has been watching him for eight
months, six days, and about three hours. In other words,
since David started high school here at Valley View
High. Right now Kael and clowns are clustered twenty
lockers down the hallway—as usual thinking David can't
hear them. One of the many things Kael doesn't know

about David is that his flesh-colored "hearing aids" are there to keep the sound *out*.

"I shouldn't have to look at that freak all day," Kael mutters. He's a short, wiry wrestler type with blond-tipped brown hair.

"His head looks like it got run over and squashed," a pal chimes in.

"His mother must have smoked crack or something."

"Maybe she drank a lot—there's that thing called feeble alcohol syndrome," Kael says.

David has been waiting for this moment. He gives his locker a major, theatrical I've-finally-had-enough slam and stalks up to Kael. Heads turn; people nudge one another. "Whoa, watch out!" somebody says.

Kael, whose father was a champion heavyweight wrestler at Valley View High not that many years ago (coaches still talk about him), straightens up his full five feet, four inches. "Hey, Stink, what's up?"

Laughter from Kael's crowd.

"It's *fetal* alcohol syndrome, you idiot," David says, "not 'feeble.' As in damage to the *fetus*. If anybody, you should know, midget." He's almost a foot taller than Kael, though he probably weighs the same.

Kael blinks several times. His pals look at one another; they're stuck on figuring out how David overheard them. David with his two hearing aids. "So, Stink, you read lips or something?" one of the clowns asks.

"Or something," David says.

Kael's neck seeps rusty red; he gets the fetal alcohol joke. He leans closer. "You know what, freak?" he says, his breath sugary rank from chewing tobacco. "Just for that I'm going to kick the crap out of you."

"You?" David says. "Or you and your feeble pals?"

"Just me. They can watch."

His gang laughs.

"Fair enough," David says. "Since you no doubt can beat me up, I should get to pick where and when—you know, like the dying prisoner's last request?"

Kael gets a blank, suspicious look; he glances, snake-like, to both sides without moving his head.

"Let him, Kael. Hey, why not?" his pals whisper.

Kael shrugs. "Okay."

"Tonight. Up on Barn Bluff, just after dark."

Kael squints.

"Unless you're afraid of heights."

"Not me, Stink."

"Middle of the bluff, north side, by the lookout over the river?"

"I know where it is. We'll be there, Crackhead. Just make sure you are."


At home at supper with the Trotwoods, his foster parents, David tries to act normal. So to speak.

"Everything all right at school today?" asks Mr. Trotwood as he passes the potatoes. Earl Trotwood has a square face with kindly blue eyes and thick farmer's hands—because he is a farmer. A hog farmer. David lives on a hog farm—a modern, industrial one with low, shiny barns off-limits to visitors, but a hog farm nonetheless. David, who grew up in New York City. (He reminds himself of this with regularity because he worries about forgetting. Forgetting the city. Forgetting his mother.) But the Trotwoods are nice people who don't pry into his personal life. They don't go through his things. He has set traps for them in his room—arranged pencils and papers just so, measured their spacing before and after—but it's clear that they don't come into his room. Not like other foster parents he has had.

When he was twelve years old, his mother sent him to Minnesota, where he would be "safe." (Safe from what? He liked New York City, its people, its neighborhoods, its smells, its food.) He first stayed with distant relatives in South Minneapolis. Really distant relatives. The parents, a biker couple, were hardly ever home, so David and his second cousins ate lots of stolen candy bars, plus pet food when they were really hungry. Canned cat food, especially Purina brand with "chicken bits," was not that bad. However, Social Services people caught up with the family, and all of the kids ended up in foster care. His mother wrote that she would come for him—but only when she got "stronger." "For now, anywhere in Minnesota is probably better than with me," she wrote. The Trotwoods, for reasons beyond David's brain, picked him out of a foster care listing of "Kids Who Wait" and brought him home.

"School? Pretty much okay," David replies. He shovels in another mouthful of food; this keeps him from having to talk.

Mr. and Mrs. Trotwood exchange a glance. In the silence, David's fork clinks loudly on his plate.

"Remember, David, the first year of high school is tough for everyone," Margaret Trotwood says. "Turning sixteen is not an easy time." She has an open face and warm blue eyes that have never looked on him with anything but kindness; he also knows that she talks to his high school counselor behind his back.

"I'll remember that, ma'am, thank you," he says, and finishes up.

After supper he tends to his homework at the dining room table, periodically checking his watch as the sun sinks lower. It's spring, April in Minnesota, and while the days are warmer, they are still short. "Darn!" he says suddenly.

"What is it, David?" Mr. Trotwood asks from his recliner.

"I forgot to do my history assignment."

"What kind of assignment?" Mrs. Trotwood asks.

"Some research on the Vietnam War," David answers.

"Can't you go online?" Mr. Trotwood asks. "You're welcome to use my office." Despite his flannel shirts and faded denim overalls, there are no flies on this hayseed: He has a souped-up Gateway computer in his office and multiple live feeds from fixed cams in his farrowing barn.

If you want to watch pig birthing or track growth curves and feed budgets, Mr. Trotwood's office is the place to be.

"We're supposed to find an actual book—so we don't forget how, Mrs. Johnson says."

The Trotwoods look at each other; that makes sense to them. "I suppose you could drive to the public library in town," Mrs. Trotwood says. "You have your farm driving permit."

"It won't take long, I promise," David says, and gathers up his things.

"Be home by nine thirty!" she calls after him. "And remember your shower tonight. Hygiene is important for growing young men."

"Yes, ma'am," he says. All his foster parents found some way to comment on his body odor, a unique scent that clung to him, resistant to all soaps and hot water. Beyond being able to drive at fifteen, the only other possible benefit to living on a hog farm was that it sometimes masked his smell. But not to Mrs. Trotwood.

"Call us if you have trouble of any kind," she hollers.

"Thank you. I will," he calls back. He feels bad lying to the Trotwoods about his evening plans, but only briefly. It's almost like they're asking for it.

# 2

For his Supreme Plan, David needs darkness and wind but not too much of either. As he drives toward town, roadside tree branches flutter in a light northwest breeze. The sun is setting. Shadows are falling in the fields, in their endless rows of finger-high corn. Perfect.

He stops at the library, slides into the history section, where he grabs a couple of books on Vietnam, then slumps down in the far corner of Periodicals to kill a few minutes. He picks up a *GQ* magazine, looks closely at the male models: their jutting, angular chins; their sharp and symmetrical cheekbones; their wide shoulders underneath thousand-dollar silk shirts. Men who turn heads. David, too, turns heads, though for different reasons. He considers defacing the models—giving each a short face, bug eyes, a stooped back like he has—but doesn't. Looking strange is one thing, being a library creep is another—and besides, the library windows have grown dusky.

He drives east out of Red Wing. At the edge of town, Barn Bluff rises up like a giant wart. Standing alone beside the Mississippi River, Barn Bluff is three hundred feet high and a close to a mile around. It was supposedly a sacred place for the Natives, and even Henry David Thoreau wrote about it on his trip up the Mississippi. In the spring, birders climb the bluff to count migrating hawks and eagles; in October people march up it in droves to take pictures of the autumn leaves that burn red and orange along the river valley. David, too, couldn't do without Barn Bluff, though for a different reason.

In the parking lot, a dozen or so vehicles idle in the shadows of the bluff. Most are Ford F-150 pickups with oversize tires driven by Carhartt-wearing, snuff-chewing "farmer" boys who will never leave this town. Here and there are short-girl cars, midsize older Chevys, Pontiacs, and Toyotas. These belong to stubby young females with ponytails pulled out the backs of their baseball caps, girls who work three jobs so they can drive around in their own cars smoking cigarettes and talking on cell phones, girls who like truck boys who chew snuff and treat them badly, girls whose lives are peaking right now only they don't know it.

He pulls up in the Trotwoods' pickup, kills the engine.

"Hey, Stink, we didn't think you were coming," Kael says, checking his watch. Rap music thumps from several pickups. What is it with white farm boys and their rap music?

David gets out. "Shall we?" he says, and points up the stone stairway to the narrow trail.

"After you," Kael says.

David takes the lead. Behind him, flashlight beams stretch out down the trail, bobbing like fireflies in the growing darkness. He doesn't need a light; he knows every bend of this path.

It takes them ten minutes to reach the top, by which time he is panting; Kael is not.

"Stink, you're out of shape, man."

"So it'll be over that much sooner," he wheezes and slumps back against a gnarly, stunted tree. The others arrive, and their flashlights gradually tighten in a circle around Kael and him. The edge—the precipice—is only a few yards behind David. He turns momentarily toward the cliff to test the northwest breeze: still good.

"No escape, dude," Kael says.

"No escape—like life itself," David says, hugging his ribs as if he is suddenly cold and afraid. In truth he is checking the sides of his Windbreaker, their discreet, vertical slits. He touches, farther inside, along his bare rib cage, his Secret of Secrets, his Trick of Tricks.

"Say what?" Kael says.

David stands up to face the group. "From death, I mean. We're all born, so at some point that means we all die."

"You're gonna die, all right," Kael says.

"Actually, you're correct," David answers (he makes his

voice go shaky and strange). "It's the reason I invited all of you up here."

Everyone is silent; flashlight beams stop moving.

"What the hell you talking about?" Kael says.

"Life's not easy for me," he begins. "The teasing, the jokes, the stares. Yes, I wear hearing aids, and yes, I'm a freaky person to look at, and sometimes I don't smell so good—"

"You got that right, whew!" Kael interrupts, fanning the air around his face (laughter from his pals).

"But deep inside me there's a normal teenager—just like any of you," David continues. He makes his voice catch, as if he's starting to break down and cry.

"This is too weird," one girl says.

"Let's get out of here," another says.

"Sorry! Too late for that!" David says. He steps sideways to block the trail.

Kael glances around—to the shadows—then back to David. He grins. "So what is this, some kind of Freddy film? The freak's revenge where you kill us all? How you going to do that, Stink?"

"I don't kill anybody," he says. "It's, well, sort of the opposite." He turns, sprints toward the edge, and dives off the cliff and into pitch darkness. The screams behind him are better than any teen slasher film—they're real.

In the parking lot, with his hands and knees slightly scratched—his landing after his long, graceful glide was a bit shaky—he hides in the bushes. He waits. It doesn't take long. In a few minutes lights bob crazily down the trail; he hears bodies crashing against bushes, boots scraping on rocks. Some kids have fallen down. There are torn jeans, bloody knees; girls are sobbing, and boys are panting in dry gasps.

"We gotta get out of here!" someone says, and they scatter for their cars.

"Wait. Nobody go anywhere. We gotta figure out what to do!" Kael shouts.

Everyone stumbles to a halt. The girls continue to sob; the guys are grim and white-faced.

"It doesn't matter what we say or do, it's gonna be our fault that he killed himself!" a girl blubbers.

Kael pauses. Thinks. "Not if we all say we were never here."

There is silence but for panting and blubbering.

"Sure—like nobody's ever gonna talk?" a girl says.

"None of us won't," Kael says. He grabs her by the hair and bends her neck sideways.

"Hey, don't, man!" says the girl's boyfriend.

"Yeah," says another. "And anyway, you were the one who was gonna fight him—"

"Yeah, it wasn't us," several voices say. "It was you." They turn on Kael even faster than David had guessed.

Kael swings his arm and points a finger that pauses briefly on each one. "You were all here. That makes you a part of this. Whoever is at the scene of a murder is guilty, too. An accessorary."

There is silence.

"So we gotta tell," someone says.

"Who?"

"The police, you idiot."

"Should I call?" a girl says. Several dig frantically for their phones, as if the first caller gets off free.

"No, wait. Maybe he's not dead," Kael says.

There is silence.

"Jesus, it's, like, two hundred feet down," someone says.

"No one could survive that," another murmurs.

"Maybe he got hung up in a tree or something."

"Yeah, that could happen," a couple of voices say quickly.

"So first we should go look for him."

"What if we find him and he's all smashed or something?"

"*Then* we can call the police."

"And we can pretend to do CPR or something until they come!" a girl says.

"Maybe you want to give that freak mouth-to-mouth," Kael mutters. "Not me."

They all scramble into their cars, fire the engines, and spin gravel as they drive off toward town—toward the other side of the bluff. Kael's Dodge Ram leads the way.

After a discreet period, David slips into the Ford and

motors away, well behind them, headlights extinguished. He follows their convoy into town and parks behind the old St. James Hotel. He peeks around a brick corner— watches their flashlights bob along the railroad tracks pinched between the Barn Bluff cliff and the Mississippi River. When they pass under the Highway 63 bridge (which crosses into Wisconsin), he skulks down across Levee Street into the shadows and follows his own search party. Farther ahead, at the base of Barn Bluff, their beams prod upward to the rocks. Sideways into the trees. Down into cold, dark, moving water.

"Hey, David!" Kael calls.

"David, dude, are you out there, man?" another says.

"David! We're sorry! We never meant anything bad to happen!" a girl whimpers.

From behind a tree he watches them beat the brush for a half hour. They shine their beams up into every tree; they stumble along in small groups, afraid of what they might find. Some of the girls are getting hysterical. He wishes he had a ghoul mask and a giant rubber ax—or else he could do a real *Blair Witch Project* on them—but he has something way subtler planned.

"There's no blood, no nothing," Kael says. His beam plays upward on the craggy side of the bluff, then down to the tracks, then finally to the river.

"He must have bounced into the water," someone says.

"Yeah, that's probably it," voices say quickly.

"And drowned."

"So he's gone, then, yes?" Kael says sharply. "The current probably took him a mile downriver by now."

"Maybe they'll never find him," someone says.

"They hardly ever find bodies in the Mississippi," Kael says.

"No body, no evidence—like on Court TV," someone says.

"There was no crime anyway, you freaking idiots," Kael says. "Tell me what the crime is."

There is silence.

"Did we touch him?"

"No."

"Did any of us lay a hand on him?"

"No," mumbles another girl.

"That's right, no one did," Kael says.

People start to get a grip. Their lights are now turned toward one another, a tightening circle of agreement.

"So we just go back to school tomorrow. Like nothing ever happened."

There is silence.

"Okay, people?" Kael says menacingly.


In the morning, David leaves for school on time but purposefully kills forty-five minutes driving around. Kael and friends are in his first-hour algebra class, and David wants them to get the full value from his empty desk.

In the giant school parking lot, he waits until the

second-period bell rings, then hurries in. He picks up a tardy slip and slinks into the crowds. Staying low, he slides along the sophomore hallway to where Kael and his friends have gathered between periods. They are circled up like buffalo in winter, grim-faced and saying nothing to anyone. Several girls are trying not to cry—all of which allows him to sneak up on them.

"Hey, gang, what time is it?" David calls. He slaps Kael hard on the back.

There are screams—louder screams than last night. Kael spins around. He stares at David, white-faced, his Adam's apple bobbing. He begins to tremble big-time.

"Gee, Kael, what's the matter?" David asks. "You look, may I say, a little freaked out."

# 3

After that, as if somebody has flushed a giant toilet, David's life at Valley View High goes rapidly down the tube. By midweek he can't pass down the sophomore hall with getting jostled and punched—secret sucker punches that double him over, make him grunt. By the following week the Trotwoods are summoned, and they all meet with Mr. Gangelhoff, the tidy, muscular, I-was-a-Marine-and-don't-you-forget-it assistant principal.

"David's presence has become disruptive to the other students. He's been in at least two fights this week, and he doesn't make any kind of effort to fit in. All that considered, we think a change of scene, a fresh start would be best for David," Mr. Gangelhoff says.

"Who is 'we'?" Earl Trotwood asks.

Gangelhoff ignores him.

"What do you mean by 'fresh start'?" Margaret Trotwood asks.

"I've made a call to Oak Leaf Alternative School," he says.

"Oak Leaf?" Margaret Trotwood says quickly. "But that's for—"

"Young people who need a more nontraditional learning environment," Gangelhoff finishes. He manufactures a smile that clangs off the rim of his mouth and dribbles away out of bounds.

"In other words," Earl Trotwood says, "you have no room for anyone who's different."

"That's not what I said. In fact, we encourage tolerance and diversity here. But our larger goal is student success," Gangelhoff says, flashing another lame smile. "And success is often all about the right environment. The right school."

After David cleans out his locker, they drive home in silence. Margaret Trotwood is sniffling, and Earl has a grim look on his face. "High school is not like it used to be," he murmurs.

"I wouldn't last a week, myself," Mrs. Trotwood agrees. "They would have pecked my eyes out."

"Now, dear," Earl says, and pats his wife on the hand. David feels bad for them, but mostly he feels nothing. At home he goes to his room and takes a long nap, while the Trotwoods call the new school and make arrangements.

When David wakes up, one of the late afternoon please-humiliate-me-and-my-family shows is on TV. He catches a segment called "Tomboy Transformation!" Parents trot out several young girls, ages nine to twelve or so, who are dressed in basic T-shirts and jeans. Normal-looking young girls. "But don't you want to look like *real* girls?" the host asks them. He is a tanned guy with big white teeth.

The girls look at one another and shrug. "I dunno, not really," one of the slim girls answers, and the crowd groans—then votes with the host by hooting and clapping loudly. The girls are herded offstage, where they will get ten-minute makeovers: new hairstyles, full makeup, trendy clothes. Great care will be taken that the girls do not see themselves in mirrors. While this goes on, the host talks to the parents, who confide that they worry their daughters might be lesbians. "They just don't seem to have no interest in boys," a fat, sloppy father says. More mindless banter with the concerned parents—and commercial breaks—give the makeover technicians time to work their magic. Finally, thumping runway music announces that the girls are ready. Everyone turns as the girls are led back onstage. They look like L.A. teen pop stars. The crowd goes wild with applause.

"Go ahead, girls, strut your stuff!" the host calls. The girls, unsteady on platform shoes, traipse across the stage like clumsy fashion models. Off to the side, the parents weep with joy.

"How do you feel?" the host presses.

The girls seem uncertain.

"Are you ready to see the new you?" he shouts.

At that moment the curtain rises on wide, full-length mirrors. The girls stumble to a halt; as they stare at their made-over selves, the crowd laughs and cheers.

"Why hide the real girl inside?" the host asks. The crowd claps and whistles its approval. The girls nod uncertainly—they have startled eyes—as their parents rush forward to embrace them. Credits roll. "Next time—cousins who marry!" shouts the host. "Good day, all!"

The following day David drives the Trotwoods' pickup for his first day at Oak Leaf Alternative School. On the long farm driveway, he meets two dusty trucks carrying men who work for Mr. Trotwood. He gives a brief wave to each, José in his Chevy and Elmer in his Dodge. Eight hours in the hog barns. Punch in, punch out. On the other hand, he would be happy to trade places with them today.

When he reaches the highway, cars whistle past him, some honking their horns. He offers them a middle-finger greeting: Day One at a new school, why should he be in a hurry?

He still feels bad about making trouble for the Trotwoods, who have been unfailingly nice to him. This old Ford F-150, for example—they let him use it as if it were his own. It has a stick shift, but Mr. Trotwood taught him how to drive it. They bucked and jerked about the farmyard as if the truck had square tires, until he got it down.

Now the Ford's clutch and shift are second nature to him, like throwing a ball, like falling into bed. The cab is strewn with his own stuff—stocking caps, notebooks, maps, books—and he hardly even notices the smells (antiseptics, minerals, salt, hog medicines). This old Ford is the one place he really feels at home.

Speaking of which, right now he could keep driving east. Cross over the Mississippi River into Wisconsin. Pick up the freeway and drive on through Chicago and all the way back to New York City. But he couldn't do that to the Trotwoods, and besides, he has all of six dollars in his pocket. He takes a deep breath, pulls his stocking cap lower over his ears, and turns in to Oak Leaf.

He parks in the far corner of the lot, away from the other cars.

Turns off the engine.

The school grounds are located west of Red Wing on an old estate called the Haroldsen Center. There's a mansion, barn, and silo next to a newer concrete-and-glass building, which is the school. There's someone standing in the foyer. A girl. She seems to be looking at the Ford, waiting for David. He doesn't get out of the truck, so she comes out of the main door of the school. She is short, wears a rainbow-colored knit cap and a long black trench coat that drags behind her. She heads directly toward him.

He pretends to be organizing his things in the cab and

to be surprised when the funky-looking girl taps on his window. He rolls the window partway down.

"Hi. Are you David?"

"Yes and no," he says. Which is the truth.

She smiles. "My name is Cheetah. I'm your student meeter and greeter." She speaks loudly.

"I can hear you fine," he says.

"Sorry," she says, glancing at his hearing aids.

He looks past her to the school grounds.

"Anyway, I like 'Yes and no,'" she says. "'Cheetah' is my personal name for myself; my given name is Megan, but I've never felt like a Megan."

He looks at her. Rolls the window down a couple more turns. "What would a Megan feel like?"

"A Megan would feel great about herself all the time. She'd be a tall blond volleyball star who plays French horn and volunteers at the rehab center and has a perfect 4.0 grade point average," Cheetah says, all the while looking at him. For some reason he doesn't mind her stare. Her eyes stay on his bug eyes; they don't move to his pinched face, his nonexistent chin. She doesn't inspect him. Measure him. Size him up. Sometimes he thinks he knows what it's like to be a girl—the way men's eyes scan their bodies up and down as if they're newspapers with headlines to be read. But she doesn't do that. Then again, her gray eyes are slightly strange, as if she has thick contact lenses or something. Maybe she just has bad eyesight.

"Plus, I like cats," she says. "I'm pretty sure I was one in a former life." She jerks her rainbow head toward the school. "Come on, David. You have to get out sometime."

He pulls his stocking cap even lower over his forehead and opens the door. On the pavement, he towers over her; she's barely five feet tall.

She looks up at him. She stands closer than most people are comfortable with in the Midwest. "So what's your story?"

He likes her manner, her smell (patchouli oil); she reminds him of people back in SoHo and the East Village. A girl not from here. "My story?" He shrugs. "I was too popular up at Valley View High. I kept winning all the awards—captain of the football and basketball teams, Prom King, Mr. Congeniality, Snow King, et cetera. I started to feel really guilty about it, so in order to give other kids a chance, I transferred here."

"Amazing! Same with me!" Cheetah says. "Come on, let's do the tour."

He lets her pull him along. No girl other than his mother has ever taken him by the arm; it's an amazing feeling—like letting go of something but receiving something more all in the same moment.

"So where you from?" she asks.

"Here," he lies.

"No, I mean, where'd you grow up?"

"Kansas," he lies.

"So how did you end up here?"

"There was this really strong west wind."

"That's cool," she says, meaning it doesn't matter. She stops, as if something else, some other thought is on the way but won't come all the way into her head, then sort of twitches and moves on as if nothing weird just happened. "The Haroldsen Center is a neat place," she continues. David pauses to look at the life-size horse sculpture made from old metal car parts, including hub-caps, axles, and wire; the horse is reared up as if pawing the air. "The old buildings, including the mansion—off-limits to us, of course—were built around 1900 by this lo-cal guy made good. He was, like, a mad scientist of some kind. He got rich on patents. His family couldn't keep up the estate, so they turned it into a nonprofit center for ed-ucation and the arts."

He watches her, smells her as she talks. Cheetah's patchouli oil keeps pitching him into his childhood, to the city, and he trails slightly behind her so he can take her scent fully into his nose.

"The tower has a spiral staircase inside and a circular walkway around the top. Professor Haroldsen used to do experiments by dropping things from it."

David looks up at the tower. It looks like a cross be-tween a silo and a witch's hat. "Can we go up there?"

"It's off-limits to kids, too."

"What's not off-limits?"

"These buildings," she says, pointing to newer, concrete-

and-glass buildings. "This part is sort of a center for the arts, plus a high school for losers like us."

"Hey, speak for yourself."

"Me?" she says easily. "I have epilepsy. I take lots of medication for seizures."

"Sorry," David mumbles.

"Actually, they're not so bad these days. Sort of like freeze-frame on a video camera, except when my camera turns back on, a couple of seconds are missing. But I can deal with that. I used to have major seizures, the grand mal kind, though they don't call them that anymore. Tonic Clonic or something—always a new name for them. Anyway, the kids at Valley View got too weirded out when I'd fall out of my desk and flap around on the floor. So here I am."

"Hey, there's a spaz in every crowd," David says, then worries he has gone over the line.

Cheetah laughs. "Spaz. That was me. My last day in regular high school I had a really bad seizure. I fell down and bit off the end of my tongue." She sticks out her tongue; it's squared off on the end, definitely shorter than normal. "When I came to, the tip was lying there like a little bloody mouse, plus I'd peed my pants. Not the coolest move for a ninth grader."

"There's this mutilation thing in California, where kids are getting their tongues split," he offers. "You know, like a snake's tongue?"

"Definitely too late for me," Cheetah says and pulls him along.

David feels some ice block deep inside his heart begin to shift, move, retract; a glacier shrinking, global warming at an insane pace. He's actually talking to a girl.

"Anyway, Oak Leaf works great for me," Cheetah continues. "I have to miss a lot of classes because I'm in this clinical study at the Mayo Clinic over in Rochester. They keep trying to figure out what's wrong with my brain, and I get free meds."

"Your brain seems okay to me."

"I wish," she says.

A shiver of current arcs through his own brain: not only talking, he might actually be flirting with her, which would be an all-time first.

"Come, David, I'll show you the classrooms."

Inside the front door, they pause before a time clock. "Attendance is up to you," she says. "Punch in, punch out. The secretary keeps track of your hours. You need a minimum of thirty hours per week. Other than that, there's no attendance policies, no permission slips."

A kid who looks like a miniature Sammy Davis, Jr., zips up to them. "Cheetah the Greeta—who's the tall dude?" He shoots out a tiny hand.

"David Anderson, meet Clevie."

Clevie and David shake hands. It's weird seeing a full mustache and goatee on a kid who looks ten years old.

"Cleveland James at your service," he says. "Welcome, Tall Dude." And without a second look he moves on, jiving, talking to anybody in earshot.

"Clevie gives new meaning to attention-deficit," Cheetah says. "Everybody here has some issue. What makes this school different from regular high school is that nobody tries to hide what's wrong with them."

David meets Max, a redheaded dreadlocked white kid. "Let's party soon," Max says, and flashes a longhorn salute.

"Max?"

"Shot his father," Cheetah says.

"Whoa. Why?"

"He was beating his mother."

"Shot him, like, dead?"

"Yes. You have parents?" Cheetah asks.

David pauses. "Sort of."

She's cool with that, and they continue the tour. Kids are moving around, passing in and out of classrooms and studios. Some are working on computers. Others are punching out, leaving for jobs. Two girls are very pregnant. David gets a few looks, but nothing serious.

"So what do you think?" Cheetah says to him.

"About what?" he says. He turns to her and can't stop himself; his eyes run down and up her body.

His first week at Oak Leaf passes smoothly. People talk to him. Or not. Clevie and Cheetah show him the ropes, tell him everything he needs to know. Friday afternoon they watch *The Full Monty* in film class. The teacher is a chirpy girl just out of college who makes a big deal about gender role reversal in the film plus issues of male body image—"being comfortable with who we are no matter what we look like." David gets a feeling the discussion is for his benefit. For the new weird kid in class. Clevie, always picking up multiple channels, shoots David a forget-about-it look. But David doesn't look up from his desk until class is over.

Afterward, Cheetah and Clevie and David sit in her Toyota in the parking lot.

"Sorry about Ms. Jones," Cheetah says.

"That was lame," Clevie agrees.

David shrugs.

"But a fun flick, yes?" Cheetah asks.

"Those English dudes were smokin' by the end," Clevie says, and snaps off a few seconds of seat dancing that shakes the little car.

"Do you mind if we go back through it? To see if I missed anything?" she asks David.

"My cue to outta here," Clevie says. "See you, suckah." He slaps David on the shoulder.

David is happy to be sitting alone with an actual girl, especially one wearing patchouli oil. Cheetah starts to retell *The Full Monty* scene by scene.

"Hey, what about the garden gnome bit?" he interrupts.

"Garden gnome?"

"When they steal it and accidentally break it? That whole Punch and Judy riff?"

She gives him a blank look. "Damn," she says. Her eyes well up with tears.

"Hey, it was a small bit," he says quickly, and describes the scene to her. When he finishes, they sit in silence.

"Plus the naked Nazi spy guy?" he adds.

She stares, then throws a brown apple core at him. They sit there for almost an hour, just hanging out. As they talk, another channel in his brain begins having Pleasantville-like daydreams: He has had an Extreme Makeover, after which he looks like a GQ model. He and Cheetah are elected senior prom king and queen at Valley View High School. Their classmates clap and cheer as the royal procession passes through a tall arch constructed of hundreds of delicate white carnations made of toilet paper.

# 4

Spring creeps upriver to Red Wing. It advances in fits and starts, like David and Cheetah's "pal-ness," their mutually agreed-upon term. They have warm, sunny days, then periods of cooler, uncertain weather. Cheetah is having trouble with her new meds, her blank spots are longer and more frequent, and her eyes look strange. But David couldn't care less. "Pal-ness" doesn't begin to cover his feelings for her. He's the happiest he has been in years, which makes him nervous. He keeps waiting for the downturn. For rain.

Which of course blows in one Monday. At lunchtime Max starts to talk. "So Janet and I were up on Barn Bluff Saturday night, and it was, like, sundown, and you're not supposed to be up on the bluff after dark, but me and Janet go up there all the time to hang out." Max's girlfriend, Janet, has a weird look on her face, as if she wishes he would shut up.

"So we caught the sunset, then stayed on until the stars

came out. It gets kind of creepy up there, but we had a little flashlight in case we got weirded out. Anyway, we were just lying back on the rocks, which stay warm after dark, and we were trying to lie still so the mosquitoes wouldn't notice us. We were watching the stars and trying to guess which ones were satellites and which ones were really stars, when I heard a rock clatter on the trail. I whispered to Janet, and we ducked down behind some brush. This guy comes walking along."

David slumps lower in his chair. He sneaks a look at Cheetah, who listens as if it's story time at nursery school. "Janet and I don't make a sound, because we think we're gonna get busted. But he passes a ways away from us, and I realize he's not old, just tall. Anyway, he goes right up to the edge of the cliff. We can see him mainly in silhouette now—it's pretty dark, but the west sky still has this kind of blue to it."

Slowly, David drops his chin, lets his hair fall forward, two dark curtains, horse blinders alongside his face.

"He just stands there, listening. He turns his head to one side, then the other, like he's listening to the whole river valley. I start to think he could hear my heartbeat, you know, like that Stephen King story—or maybe it was Edgar Allan Poe, where the old man is buried under the floor but his heart is still beating?"

" 'The Tell-Tale Heart,' " Cheetah says. She has read everything.

Max doesn't hear her. "So then he takes off his shirt

and tucks that in his fanny pack. Then he lifts up his arms and starts to shake them, like some kind of loosening up exercise, except that he's got these hang-glider or kite-type things attached to them. That's the only way I can describe it. Like a kite. One on each arm. Arm kites, attached to the undersides of his arms and alongside his rib cage. When he held his arms straight out sideways, this material stretched down from his wrists almost to his hips and made a triangle. Two triangles, I mean, one under each arm. The fabric was so thin we could see starlight through it. Right, Janet?"

Janet won't say anything.

"And here's the really weird part," Max says. "The guy jumps."

There is silence in the little, humid cafeteria.

"Like, off the cliff?" Clevie asks.

"Yes!" Max says; he turns to Janet.

Clevie rolls his eyes.

"It's true," she murmurs. "He jumped. I saw him. We were paralyzed. We couldn't believe it. Then we bolted back down the hill to the car—I was crying and running—'cause I thought for sure we just saw some guy kill himself."

"I said we should call 911," Max said, "but then Janet said they'd make us pee in a cup or something." (Everyone laughs.)

"So what'd you do then?" Clevie asks.

"It took us a while to decide, but then we drove around

to the river side of the bluff. You know, just to look," Janet says.

"But there was nothing," Max continued. "No one at all. He was gone."

"So he just sailed away? Like Dumbo the Flying Elephant?" Clevie says with a laugh.

"Or maybe one of the Flying Elvi," Cheetah adds.

"You better lay off that funny tobacco," Clevie says to Max and Janet.

When the subject finally changes, David slips out the door to the parking lot.

Clevie tags along, but when he sees Cheetah approaching, he stops short of David's truck. "Nudge and a wink," he says, jerking his chin toward Cheetah, and slips away.

Cheetah joins David in the Ford. "That was a really weird story," she says.

"Whatever they were smoking up there can't be good for the brain," he says.

Cheetah has brought her lunch along, in a spotted, well-wrinkled brown paper bag. His lunch pail contains the usual full meal; today it's fried chicken, coleslaw, bread and butter. He makes a show of eating but can barely taste the food. After lunch they have Study Skills Lab together, which means some downtime in the library. They find adjoining computer stations.

"Want to see something?" David says suddenly to Cheetah. He is online.

"Depends." She rolls her chair toward his monitor.

"WeirdWorldNewz.com," he answers. "It has this section on human monsters." A pop-up flashes on the
screen: "Send in your weird newz—win a trip to Can-
cún!" David quickly closes out the flashing box, then
goes to the photo gallery. The images are black-and-white
stills stolen from medical textbooks. They show all manner of deformities.

"Ick," Cheetah says, squinting her eyes as she looks at
the screen. "The site, I mean, not the kids."

"Hey, you can learn stuff here," David says. "Paganini,
the famous Italian violinist?"

"I've heard the name."

"He had these amazing fingers—like, twice as long as
most people's, and double-jointed besides. Now doctors
say he had this rare condition called Ehlers-Danlos syndrome."

Cheetah doesn't reply. David watches her stare at the
photos of naked kids, twisted and bent; some are small,
dead fetuses, but many are alive—teenagers with body
hair. With backward legs, fish-scale skin, duplicate organs
hanging on the outsides of their chests. "Look at their
eyes," David says.

Cheetah leans forward, then quickly turns away. "You
shouldn't look at freak sites like that."

"Why not?"

"They're sad, that's why."

"Hey, I'm just interested in birth defects. Say you're
born with spina bifida, or elephantiasis, or something

even weirder—you're one of those one-in-ten-zillion cases. How do you explain that?"

"Bad karma?"

David is silent. "I must have been, like, an ax murderer in a previous life."

"I was kidding!" Cheetah says, and touches his arm.

"Well if it's not bad karma, give me another explanation."

Cheetah thinks. But not for long. "To start, how about all the toxic chemicals in our environment? Like mercury in the water, like Agent Orange in the soil in Vietnam, where there are now thousands of deformed people?"

"Possibly," David says.

"Then there's drugs, legal and illegal, like that whole thalidomide thing from the sixties where babies had fish arms and duck feet—plus nowadays mothers who use crack or meth, or who drink."

David looks away.

"And what about families who have some genetic thing? Like, the parents have bad eyes so the kids need Coke-bottle glasses—that sort of thing, only worse," Cheetah continues. "Birth defects don't have anything to do with karma."

David shrugs. He is not convinced.

"And anyway, back to Paganini," Cheetah says.

"What about him?"

"If Paganini wasn't born with extra-long fingers, he wouldn't have become Paganini the famous violinist."

David has no answer for that.

"In other words, his defect was a gift," she adds.

"What about your seizures?" David shoots back. There's an odd anger in his voice. "Tell me how they're a gift."

She stares at him; slowly her gray eyes fill with glassy water. She turns away.

"I'm sorry," he begins.

"Forget it!"

"Cheetah, I'm really sorry. I didn't mean—"

"Just stop looking at that weird shit online and help me with my geometry."

He closes out the site, then goes through her problems with her one by one. Step by step. Geometry is not that difficult; it's about angles and degrees that eventually all add up, completely unlike his life so far.

# 5

A cockroach creeping across his pillow means he is dreaming. He is back in New York City. With his mother! They are living off Grand Street on the Lower East Side.

Attracted to the smell of formula on his breath, the roach creeps closer and closer. Six spiny, hesitant legs. A pair of long, nervous antennae. Two blank, bug eyes. A mouth with chewing parts.

How large he becomes! David is more fascinated than afraid, and way quicker. He crunches the roach between his pink and toothless gums; hot bug juice floods his mouth. It tastes salty, and with flavors like tobacco and wild berries. But his pleasure is interrupted. His mother cries out—snatches him from his warm blankets—jams a skinny, white finger in his mouth. She works it roughly about to expel the roach, but too late. David has swallowed it.

She clutches him to her thin breast, and they begin to cry

together. *He wails because she has scared him. She sobs from every mother's greatest fear: Her baby is not right.*

*She has noticed weird things about him from the start. His short face and wide-set eyes. These the doctors blamed on the long labor, the difficult birth, the pressures of the birth canal upon his skull. But what about the loose folds of skin in his little red armpits? Peculiar, yes, the doctors say, but all babies are wrinkled to begin with—and these things usually go away with time.*

*However, as months pass, her baby's odd looks become more pronounced, the flaps of skin under his arms grow larger. And now this—this thing with bugs. He remembers the salty taste of her tears.*

*Because of medical expenses—the endless examinations, the poking and prodding and measuring—their apartments become smaller and darker. But the shabbier their apartment, the richer its insect life. Silverfish, termites, common houseflies, crickets, spiders, roaches—none are safe from his quick, pudgy fingers.*

*He remembers the first time he heard insects. Whenever he lay quietly in his crib he was puzzled by the faint, continual whispering around him. Tiny voices he could not quite distinguish, like a radio tuned between stations and just beyond earshot. But one day he was crawling on the floor and paused to put his ear against the wall. Suddenly he heard them! Insects moving behind the plaster and lath, moving inside the cupboards, along the molding, a whole universe of them, chewing, chafing their furry legs, brushing their hairy antennae, rustling their papery wings, speaking and calling out and arguing in their subsonic tongues.*

David shifts on his pillow, almost losing the dream. Goose down, its faint crackling sigh as the feathers compress under his head, brings it back.

*He hears insects everywhere, and he can distinguish them immediately by their sounds. The softest scritching, the faintest scratching—each sound is familiar. Centipedes and millipedes are the quietest, the most difficult to identify by ear. But he can hear the endless, marching columns of their feet, and the muted, oily click of their segmented bodies as they hump along. He becomes a hunter, an omnivore on four little legs: he waits for anything that rustles in the lower cupboards, that buzzes or flutters in the air, that dares skitter across the cracked kitchen tiles.*

*To break him of eating bugs, his mother brings him more and more outside into the fresh air. He is bundled, of course, and wears oversize baby hats so people won't stare. On Saturdays they sometimes take the M9 bus to Battery Park, then ride the ferry to Staten Island and back, standing as far forward in the boat as they can—as if the salt breeze and sunlight will wash away his defects. Might cleanse their bad luck. Other days he rolls along, clack-clack, clack-clack, in his stroller over the unending seams of the sidewalks. Through a forest of knees. Old people are*

*kindest to him; they reach down to touch his head. Bless
him. He is already wearing his "hearing aids"—perhaps
the passersby feel sorry for such a child. Their suddenly
looming faces, their funny accents and greetings, the smell
of coffee or cigarettes on their breath. A stream, a river, an
unending current of people, all flowing somewhere, then
back.*

*Above knees and heads are dark brick buildings hung
with a webbing of iron fire escapes and drainpipes and
iron grillwork and clotheslines. He loves cornices and iron
scrollwork—sometimes reaches out his little fists as if to
grab them and hang on.*

*And on they roll. Smells and voices change. Occasion-
ally there are breaks in the forest of knees. Patches of blue
sky into which skyscrapers soar. So few of the blue-sky days,
though. Mostly Mom brings him out after dark.*

*Her favorite skyscraper by night is the Woolworth Build-
ing. Its lighted flying buttresses and soaring pinnacles and
spooky gargoyles and stone carvings stop her every time.
She stands there, staring up until he fusses; then she rolls
him on.*

*Another of her favorite buildings, in the opposite direc-
tion, uptown, is the Chrysler Building. The whole building
looks like a giant spear pointed into the sky. As she walks
endlessly, he sometimes cries with hunger. Then his mother
rolls him hurriedly through side streets, his stroller wheel-
ing faster—chuckachuckachucka—on old bricks and cob-*

blestones, where new smells and noises rise up. Soon he has a bagel to chew on, or a sour pickle to suck, and he is happy again.

As is his mother. At least somewhat. In the night, free of their tiny, dark apartment, a youngish woman with baby in stroller, they go everywhere—into neighborhoods where men sprawl on concrete stoops. Where matches flare inside their cupped hands. Where tiny bonfires burn in empty lots. Men call out hoarsely as they approach:

"Hey, honey, where you going? Hey, sister, over here."

"Qué pasa, mamacita? What you doin' here? You strung out? Or you just loco? Go on home, now!"

But they pass safely by. His mother with her pale skin and fine bones and dark hair and sad eyes, as beautiful as Madonna. The real Madonna, of course. And with her baby (perhaps he helps keep her safe!) she may be almost Holy.

"Up and at 'em, Dave-eeee!" Earl Trotwood calls from downstairs. It's morning in Minnesota, and Earl's high tenor voice, sharpened by years of hog calling, penetrates David's pillow like a lightning strike through a telephone wire. He jerks upright in bed—quickly straps on his "hearing aids" before Mr. Trotwood calls again.

6

"Don't want to have to call the undertaker!" Mr. Trotwood adds, his voice booming up the stairway.

"Alive and well, sir," David calls, letting one foot fall out of bed and thump onto the floor. It is their usual exchange on schoolday mornings, and not an unpleasant one.

The time is, of course, 7:00 a.m. Exactly. Mr. Trotwood's punctuality, his precision, is annoying, but so far David has few complaints about his foster parents. Earl and Margaret Trotwood are religious but not severe or conservative in their beliefs. They believe in issues of social justice—they're probably Democrats—and in general are optimistic, charitable, and tolerant (all of which David is not). Their "ministry" in life, as Mrs. Trotwood calls it, is to provide a home for kids who need one. That would be him.

He brushes back his hair, puts on his glasses and stock-

ing cap (he keeps no mirror in his room), and heads
downstairs for breakfast.

"Morning, David."

"Morning, sir."

The television is on, muted as usual.

"I noticed your light rather late last night," Mrs. Trotwood says.

"Doing some homework, ma'am."

"I tapped on the door, but it was locked."

"Sorry, I must have fallen asleep reading."

Earl Trotwood clucks his tongue. "Remember, son, a
growing lad needs plenty of rest."

"And a good breakfast to start the day," Margaret Trotwood adds; she sets a wide plate of bacon, eggs, and pancakes before him.

"Thank you, ma'am."

The Trotwoods' only character flaws show up on Sun-
days in church (he goes mainly to please them; it's not
too much to ask), where they make a fuss about how well
their "newest child" (they have none of their own) is getting on. The Trotwoods like to say they have "no children
but many children." They have won awards for their
charity and are thought of, his social worker let slip, as a
family "of last resort." This means they will take any kid,
no matter what his problems. Before landing with the
Trotwoods, David stayed with several other Minnesota
families, none of which worked out. ("There's just something about David that gave my wife the willies . . .")

"Everything going all right at Oak Leaf?" Mr. Trotwood asks.

"Yes, sir. Going very well."

"We're proud of you, David," Mr. Trotwood says, straightening his cap at the front door. "Mrs. Trotwood and I just want you to know that."

"Thank you, sir."

Mr. Trotwood tells David this nearly every morning before school, and it's a cheesy moment, but it gets David every time—and Mr. Trotwood, too. The farmer's Adam's apple bobs and his eyes shine suddenly rounder and more luminous. He can well up with tears faster than any man David has ever known; David has learned never to get him started on the old days and the Shetland pony he once had.

"Well, it's off to the office, dear," he says to Mrs. Trotwood.

She laughs dutifully. The "office" in this case is the pig barn, wherein he actually has a nice office. Mr. Trotwood's barns are long, low, air-conditioned, and nearly automated (lucky for David, who has only light chores on the farm grounds). He has been in the barns just once, for a tour, which required high rubber boots, fresh white coveralls, and a surgical-type face mask. "Not for you, for the hogs," Mr. Trotwood explained. He is big on preventing disease; there are boot dips at every door, and the buildings are sealed against airborne viruses. Inside, the sound of hundreds of hogs was amazing. Their smell, like very rotted cheese, did not bother David. He could work in the barns if he had to.

Today, Earl gives Mrs. Trotwood a crisp salute and departs.

Then it's just Margaret Trotwood and David in the kitchen, with the flashing television as the mute third party. "You know, David, I've been thinking," she says, beginning to bustle about, making slightly more noise with her pots and pans now that they are alone (the willies effect). "You're getting so tall—have you considered trying out for the high school basketball team?"

"You mean, like, regular high school?" David knows that students at Oak Leaf are entitled to participate in sports and extracurriculars at Valley View High, although none do.

"Yes, David. Valley View High. I know you had trouble there, but, well, you're getting to be such a man now." She colors slightly.

David is antsy. He has the peculiar idea that she is gearing up for a talk with him about the birds and bees.

"I don't really like basketball, ma'am. I think I'm more the . . . artistic type." In fact, David thinks he might be quite good at basketball or even baseball—but there is the small matter of the sports physical. He has not been to a physician since his toddler days. He has taken great pains to avoid seeing a doctor ever again. One of his recurring bad dreams (he has it at least once a week) is to wake up in a hospital examining room, naked.

"Well, never say never, David," Margaret says with some relief. She is already washing his empty breakfast plate. "Still, it's too bad you can't go to regular high school."

He pauses.

"You know what I mean, David," she says quickly. "I know Oak Leaf is good for, well, certain kids. You know, the ones who can't get along, or have problems, but you're such a nice young fellow. Mr. Trotwood and I have found you nothing but a pleasure." She blurts the last part, as if it has come as a surprise to them.

"And I you, ma'am," he says. As he sets his empty orange juice glass within reach, he pats her shoulder.

She immediately clamps onto his hand with her warm, wet, dishwater fingers and squeezes tightly. It's a shame she had no real children; she would have been a wonderful mother. In a flash of insight, David sees that it's not her fault she has no children: Mr. Trotwood is to blame. That's the reason he's so outgoing and optimistic but prone to tears: he is a man without seed. Every kind thing he does for his wife is some kind of compensation, some small apology.

"Tsk, tsk, Davy," she says as she examines his fingers. "You should use hand lotion. Girls hate chapped hands, you know."

He manufactures a laugh and pulls away.

"Did you have your shower today?"

"Yes!" he says with annoyance.

He feels guilty about their relationship; he should say
more to Mrs. Trotwood, tell her things—he has lived
here eight months already—but he just can't, so they
stick with routine exchanges, predictable words. Mrs.
Trotwood will never be his real mother.

Who in the last few weeks has become slightly out of fo-
cus in his mind's eye. Just out of reach in some region of
his heart. Is this because of Cheetah? Are his feelings for
her pushing away memories of his mother? That this
could *even* be the case darkens his mood like a can of
black paint spilled inside his head, like an oil slick
spreading across his brain. He returns to his room, un-
locks his little square desk safe, and takes out a photo. It is
tattered and fuzzy at the edges, like a well-used baseball
card. In the photo his mother is wearing cat's-eye sunglasses and a summer dress. The Statue of Liberty is behind them. They are on the Staten Island ferry. She is
wearing a blue scarf. He has on his sunglasses and a cap
pulled down and is holding her hand. She is very thin but
smiles into the camera, which she must have handed to a
stranger. It was always just the two of them. David knows
nothing about a father.

He reaches deeper into the little safe and takes out the
blue scarf. The very same one. He closes his eyes. Buries
his face in the thin liquid of her silk. His mother hasn't
written him for over a year.

# 7

At school he tries to be Mr. Cheerful with Ms. Cheetah, but she picks up on his gloominess and makes it her own, times two. Mood theft. Nothing more annoying in a relationship—if that's what this can be called. Going out? Sort of. Going steady? No. Going crazy? Yes. He is dumbstruck, brain-addled, tongue-twisted in love. Clevie airmics Frank Sinatra love songs whenever he sees Cheetah and David together, and Max flashes double longhorn salutes. As the song goes, "Everybody Knows," including Ms. Jones, the overly cheerful English teacher, who thinks it's "so sweet" that David and Cheetah have hooked up.

Sickening, is what it is. Literally. David forgets to check in, forgets to check out, forgets assignments, forgets to eat his lunch, which gives him a headache, and forgets to drink water, which leaves him dehydrated and depressed. His adviser calls him in to go over his time card (Clevie and Cheetah vouch for his attendance), and David promises to get a grip ("Remember, Oak Leaf is all about personal responsibility," his adviser warns). But he spends a lot of time staring out his classroom windows—which on the following day is a good thing. Kael Grimes's red pickup rumbles into the Oak Leaf parking lot.

David jerks upright in his chair. The cab of Kael's Dodge Ram is filled with wrestlers. He brakes by David's Ford, gives it a long look, then sprays gravel with his tires as he turns back toward the highway. David lets out a breath.

"Friends of yours?" Max asks, leaning out from a computer carrel.

David glances over his shoulder; Max keeps popping up these days. David has this odd sensation that Max is watching him.

"Not me," David says. "You know them?"

Max squints after Kael's truck. "Nope. Never seen them before," he says, and turns back to his computer screen.

David sneaks a last look at Kael's departing taillights. Damn. What part of stupid allowed him to think that Kael would forget about his Barn Bluff humiliation? Wrestlers get points just for hanging on.

"David, dude, you're looking a little white—if you get my drift," Clevie says. He's passing; he's always passing, but David doesn't mind Clevie. "You see a ghost or something?"

"No. Just thinking about stuff." David sees Max turn slightly sideways so as to listen.

"No future in that," Clevie says. "Right, Maxie?"

"Huh?" Max says, pretending to be busy.

After Clevie moves on, David continues to stare out the window. Kael will return—no doubt about that—and David starts thinking of ways to not be in school.

On Tuesday his prayers are answered. Sort of. Cheetah comes up to him in the hallway. "I have to go to the Mayo Clinic tomorrow, want to come?"

"Are you all right?" he asks quickly.

"It's that epilepsy study I told you about. I need to check in there once a month to stay qualified for free meds."

"Sure, I'll go," he says. He hunches his shoulders slightly.

"Or not," she says. "It's not like you have to."

"I want to come," he says. "It's just . . . hospitals."

"What about them?"

"I think I have a hospital phobia."

"Hey, it's me who has to see a doctor. All you'd have to do is drive me and hang out for a couple of hours."

"No problemo," he says, too cheerfully.

"Neither of my parents could get away. The doctors dilate my pupils and do other weird stuff, so I need somebody to drive me back," Cheetah says.

"I'm there. I'm a driving fool."

Cheetah gives him an annoyed look, but the gig is on.

The next morning they punch out of school at 10:00 a.m.
They fill Cheetah's car with gas at the Oasis quick-stop,
where David buys some snacks and the latest print edition of *Weird World Newz*.

"Not that again," Cheetah says.

"Hey, it's important to keep up on current events," he
says. They head through town, Cheetah driving, and turn
south on Highway 58. Barn Bluff, with its crumbling
painted-stone American flag, stares down at the town;
Cheetah doesn't look up at it, and David says nothing.
Let sleeping bluffs lie. South of town they drive past the
giant Valley View High School. High on a hill, a sprawl-
ing campus of new yellow brick buildings with high,
curving walls.

"Shawshank High," David says.

Cheetah laughs and cranks up the music. The interior
of her car smells like a girl—hand lotion and patchouli
and cream rinse and other, secret things—all of which
makes him horny. Aroused. He shifts in the seat and
keeps his tabloid over his lap. Being in Cheetah's little
car is like being in her bedroom, which might happen
when the United States has a Green Party president.

In the countryside there are blushes of new yellow-
green along the bases of south-facing, smaller bluffs,
though the trees higher up are still bare. The sun is shin-

ing on farm country; there is the smell of fresh manure in the air.

"I usually go with one of my parents," Cheetah shouts over some hard-driving punk rock. "They flip a coin; loser has to take me."

"Not true," he shouts back.

"It is true," she replies. He knows only a little about her parents: Cheetah's father has had several jobs, none more than a few years, and her mother, a chain smoker, sells Mary Kay beauty products and falls for every pyramid scheme that comes along. On the phone her mother's voice is hoarse and smoky-sounding; her father's is thin and uncertain. David has never spoken with them in person.

He rustles open the *Newz*, scans the pages. The cover article is about a "wild child" found in Borneo. "Want to hear an article?" he asks Cheetah.

"Not really."

"Just one—it's short. 'Wild Child of Borneo'?"

"All right, all right."

David reads her the story about the "wild child" captured by outlaw teak loggers. The hairy kid has perfect teeth and a language all its own. Observed several times by the loggers, it always escaped with gazellelike speed, but was captured only when its ankle-length hair became entangled in a thornbush.

"Sad," Cheetah says.

"Wait, there's more," David says. "Great touch here at

the end: 'Wild Child's amazing hair found to carry data better than fiber-optic cables—making him a true Miracle Boy. Loggers, fearful of offending the Forest Gods, set him free.' "

"I would hope," Cheetah says.

As they get closer to Rochester, Cheetah gradually turns down the music. One notch about every ten miles. By the time they enter the north side of town, they aren't listening to any music. In silence they pass a sign: WELCOME: ROCHESTER POP. 97,000.

"Welcome to City of the Sick," Cheetah says.

David looks around. Newer suburban sprawl, auto lots, shopping malls. His stomach has its Tweety Birds as he thinks about hospitals, their smells, their doctors in white coats, but he fakes a yawn. "Looks like a fairly normal town to me."

"You'll see," Cheetah says.

They turn off Highway 52 onto Civic Center Drive, then through some side streets toward the tallest buildings and the city center. He starts to see motel signs: LONG-TERM STAY OK and BY THE WEEK WITH KITCHENETTES and FREE SHUTTLE TO MAYO.

" 'Transplant House'?" David says suddenly, turning his head toward a nicely kept old brick home.

"Where you'd stay if you were waiting for a transplant," Cheetah says.

"Duh," David answers.

Then, suddenly, the Mayo complex of buildings rises up. The marquee of the actual Mayo Building is aluminum and curving and art deco, like parts of the Chrysler Building made by midgets. These buildings are only twenty or so stories, not one hundred, and they are full of sick people. And injured people. And dying people. So many that they spill out onto the sidewalks in their walkers, or sit in wheelchairs where the sun is striking as if the warm rays will save them or set them free.

Cheetah stops the car before a crosswalk filled with white-coated doctors and nurses in flowery smocks and tennis shoes.

"Rochester would be a great place to have a heart attack or get run over," David says. "Doctors would fight over you."

Cheetah doesn't answer. Her jaw is clenched. At the next crosswalk she brakes for a group of Arabs; the men wear long white robes and colorful head wraps, the women black veils and gowns. A culture of black and white. They push along the wheelchair of a younger, handsome keffiyeh-wearing man who sits erect but tilted; in the sunlight his skin is a dark sunflower yellow. He wears sunglasses and does not turn his head. He looks frozen. Taxidermied.

"Saudis," Cheetah says. "They fly to the Mayo Clinic if they get a head cold. They have entire wings of the hospitals reserved just for them."

"That dude has more than a head cold," David says. He glances at Cheetah; she's not one to diss people because of what they look like or where they come from.

"All I'm saying is Mr. Sheikh there is gonna get way better health care than some single mother in Rochester who has to work two jobs to pay for her kids' day care."

David is silent.

Cheetah turns in to a parking ramp, finds a spot on the fourth level, and shuts off the engine. They sit for a moment in silence. "Sorry," she says.

"About what?"

She shrugs. "I sorta hate coming here."

"Hey, in and out," he says, "me and you."

She smiles and gives him a quick hug. "Come, I know all the shortcuts."

They get out of the car, cross the ramp, and cut through the fourth floor of the Kahler Hotel, which looks as if it has been around a few years. The corridors are dim, with faded pastel colors; there's a walker or a wheel-chair parked by about every third door. Room service breakfast trays have been set outside for pickup. Most are loaded with leftover food; one tray has a major breakfast that looks totally untouched. Cheetah glances at David, he at her; she grabs the banana, he two croissants plus butter squares and jelly.

"Nobody here eats much," he whispers.

"They're all dying," Cheetah whispers back.

They take the elevator, a narrow but handsome old

kind, empty except for Cheetah, David—and faded mirrors. David's brain contracts into a walnut, a piece of
coal, deflates like a balloon, sputters to the floor, lies
there dead. Mirror shock: it happens on the rare occa-
sions that he forgets what he looks like and then stumbles
upon a looking glass. Peering back at him is a stooped,
skinny teenager with a small face and overly large eyes
partially disguised behind heavy, black-framed glasses.
Two lank curtains of hair that he can swing shut in an instant. Anyone can see that he is strange. The Wild Child
of Borneo could be his cousin.

*Ding!* One floor down, the elevator bell breaks the bad
spell; he and Cheetah shuffle backward as a family en-
ters, two parents with a kid in a wheelchair. The kid is
about ten years old with a face bloated like a Macy's
Thanksgiving Day Parade balloon. He (she?) has an IV
bag hanging on a pole and might be dozing but it's hard
to tell because his (her?) eyes are little snake slits.

"Hi there," the mother says brightly to them.

"Hi," Cheetah says.

David nods.

The wheelchair kid turns his face toward David. "Hey."

David nods.

"So what's wrong with you?" the kid says.

"Brandon, really!" the boy's mother says.

"It's okay," David says.

Brandon the wheelchair boy keeps staring as he waits
for David's answer.

"An Extreme Makeover gone extremely wrong."

Brandon gets the joke. He laughs and wheezes so hard that his IV pole rocks and his bag threatens to fall off.

"Brandon!" his mother says. The parents have dark, raccoonlike circles under their eyes, and their faces are very pale, as if they haven't been outside for weeks.

The elevator slides downward in silence except for Brandon's raspy giggles. Then *Ding!* and the door slowly slides open again at the next floor. Two men in their thirties are waiting for a ride. They have close-cut hair and are dressed well, but one is leaning on an aluminum walker. He is as skinny as a crow, wears a white surgical-type mask, and has purple leeches—sores, actually—on his neck and face.

The healthy one of the pair pauses by the open door. "Do you mind?" he says to them, the faintest note of apology in his voice.

"Please—come on in," says the cheerful mother.

"Of course," the father says, and moves Brandon's wheelchair farther back.

Brandon squints at the man with the walker. "So what's wrong with you?"

"Brandon," his mother says tiredly.

The skinny man smiles behind his mask. "Everything, kid. Pretty much everything."

"Me, too," Brandon says. He holds up a puffy hand, and the guy with the walker does the same; they do a weak high five. As the elevator continues downward, no one says anything, but the silence is not uncomfortable. There is only the faint, faraway grinding sound of the elevator's cable and the slight rasp of breathing from Brandon and the thin man. David stares at the purple lesions on the man's neck, then turns again to look into the dim, smoked glass. Crowded together, they are a family of strangers. All of them hanging by an iron thread. All of them in this together. All of them falling. By the time they reach the first-floor lobby, David feels the burn of tears in his eyes, feels some insane kind of joy.

In the wide foyer of the Mayo Clinic, banks of wheelchairs wait, arranged by color. Yellow for radiology, blue for physical therapy, red for orthopedics, and black ones without labels. David cranes his neck up toward the ceiling of the giant lobby, the sculpture of a towering naked guy wearing a fig leaf. They take an elevator to the eighth floor, Neurology, where Cheetah checks in for her appointment. The waiting room is the size of the Oak Leaf auditorium. David lingers to the side, pretending to look at the magazines (*Reader's Digest, Field & Stream, Good Housekeeping, Ladies' Home Journal*, all current but already well-thumbed and tattered at the corners); he has this illogical fear that his own name will be called.

"Like a real hospital phobia?" Cheetah says.

"Not really," he lies.

"Think of it like being in church," she says. "Just think happy thoughts and no one will mind-meld with you or steal your brain."

They take a seat on the padded benches in the far back and, as in church, find themselves speaking in hushed voices. "At least an hour before they'll call me," Cheetah says.

"Hey, no problem," David says instantly.

She smiles and leans against him. After a while he eases his arm around her. She tilts her neck and lets her head rest on his shoulder. She is quiet, and within a minute her breathing slows. He risks a look downward; her eyelids have drooped. As she dozes against him, his arm begins to prickle and needle—it too is falling asleep—but he wouldn't move it for a million bucks.

With his free hand he reads his *Weird World Newz*. If not here, where?

When Cheetah's name is finally called, David shakes his dead arm alive and goes exploring. He takes an elevator (more wheelchairs and aluminum walkers) to Subway Level. There the door opens to the City of the Sick.

Clutching charts and X-rays, the ill and injured move along airportlike concourses with three-legged canes, with walkers, with wheelchairs, with electric carts. A black-dressed family of Amish passes; the men wear wide, dark hats and follow a stern, white-bearded elder driving a silent electric vehicle. Behind the Amish are two very short African women in bright robes; one has bandages

across her face and nose; the other has both hands missing, lopped off at the wrists. Next passes a young American soldier in a wheelchair, her mouth drooped open,
eyes fixed forward, the right side of her head bandaged
but very flat; both her legs are gone, too. On the plus
side, she has a half dozen bright ribbons and shiny med-
als pinned to her uniform.

Overtaking the patients are fast-striding doctors and
nurses. The nurses wear chirpy tennis shoes; the doctors
have silent shoes and guarded eyes, as if they are worried
someone might ask them something. The nurses smile
and turn toward one another to chatter about their kids,
school programs, weekend plans. They are much better
at leaving death behind than the stiff, distant doctors,
who carry death with them.

To the side, a library and reading room catches David's
eye: MAYO CLINIC PATIENT EDUCATION CENTER. In the
middle of the little library is a mannequin made of clear
plastic: a see-through man, arms held upward, complete
with all his organs. David goes inside for a closer look.
There is a front desk, as in a library, and a tidy man at
work on a computer. David inspects "Transparent Man,"
his official name (he was made for the World's Fair in
Chicago, 1933, the plaque reads). He is perfectly propor-
tioned, about six feet tall. His organs—including liver,
kidneys, bladder, heart, and lungs—are color-coded to a
chart nearby. Press a button, the pancreas lights up. Press
another and the heart pulses. David tries all the buttons.

He looks closely at the brain; it has tiny Christmas-tree-like lights flashing serially along thin wires. Neurons. Synapses. He thinks of Cheetah.

Beyond Transparent Man and to the left are more life-size plastic models of the human torso, these showing the various layers of the human body. The poor guy ("Peeled Man"?) goes from epidermis to muscles to organs (heart, lungs, and liver), all the way down to bare rib cage and spine. To the right of Peeled Man are long reading tables and beyond them shelves full of medical books and journals. At one table is a youngish, puffy-faced woman with no eyebrows and a bright scarf wrapped around her head. Alongside her is a stack of books with the word *Oncology* visible on most of the spines. She pages steadily through the biggest book, the pages making a rhythmic *shuh . . . shuh* sound.

To the right side of the room are computer terminals and shelves of DVDs and videotapes with popular titles such as *Understanding Kidney Failure* and *Schizophrenia and Your Family*. David had thought to find a quiet place to finish his *Weird World Newz* in private, but instead he cruises the shelves. He bypasses ten-facts-for-the-complete-idiot types of titles, but among them are serious medical texts. In the M's, under *musculoskeletal*, he notices a thick brick of a book: Kleinfelder's *Patterns of Human Malformation*, 9th edition. He glances again over his shoulder—the woman has not looked up from her oncology books—and hoists the book off the shelf and into a reading carrel. It's an A–Z book of birth abnormalities complete with photos:

**Angelman syndrome:** ". . . jerky, puppetlike movements, late development of motor skills, small head size (microcephaly), seizures, drooling, minimal to no speech. Also characterized by light skin, eyes, and hair color and happy, smiling behavior." So why not call it Stupid Angel syndrome?

**Apert syndrome:** "Characterized by skull malformation, syndactyly of hands and feet, mid-digital hand mass with a single nail common to digits 2 through 4." He looks at a hand composed of a thumb and one giant fingernail. Always a great way to impress the girls.

**Arthrogryposis:** "Children with arthrogryposis may have clubfoot, wrists in extension, and 'clubbed' hands with the thumb in palm, internally rotated shoulders, elbows that cannot be bent." In other words, arms frozen in place—and not a great place.

**Ehlers-Danlos syndrome** (aha, this one he knows): ". . . hyperextensibility of the skin and joints, elasticity of dermis." He leans closer; a fine-print footnote mentions Paganini, but there are no photographs of his fingers. This is disappointing; David imagines them darting about a violin neck like octopus tentacles.

**Langer-Giedion syndrome:** ". . . low ears, pinched nose, funnel-like facial features." The poor sod in the photo is even uglier than he is.

He skips along in the book. Some of the abnormalities

have classic Greek names, such as Proteus syndrome (footnote information: Proteus was a sea god famous for changing shapes). Others names are long and Latinate, with root words that can be mostly figured out, such as unilateral renal agenesis micropenis. At least he doesn't suffer from micropenis problems.

**Rett syndrome:** "Neurological disorder affecting mostly females; microcephaly, later loss of motor skills, and often characterized by hand-wringing." Hand-wringing! This is what normal people do when their whole family is killed by a tornado or a car bomb, when life can't get any worse. Some of these disorders are bad jokes on a cosmic level.

He glances at Oncology Woman (still paging) and turns to the index in the rear of the book. He scans down the alphabetized fine print, the columns. He does not know what he is looking for. *Icthyosis vulgaris* (and variants). His finger pauses: something to do with birdlike and ugly? Turning back to the *I*'s in the text, he looks at a fetus (dead) that has scaly, baggy skin—twice as much as needed, and badly upholstered. God had to have been drunk or stoned when He made that child—or maybe He just wanted to punish him. No wonder David has trouble going to church. He is about to slam shut the book and go get a candy bar when his eyes fall to the bottom of the Icthyosis Variants page, to tiny footnotes. They refer to related cases and issues involving "dermis redundance" (extra skin?): "See also study by Akbar, Ramaswamy, and

Wisman; Beth Israel Medical Center, New York, New York, 1987–90."

His limbs go arthrogrypotic (is that a word?); his body freezes in place. Beth Israel Medical Center. Not only that, there is something familiar about those doctors' names—some echo, some call, some faraway note that vibrates in his head. Hospital images—the bright lights, the smell of medicines, clear alcohol in jars and then in cotton swabs suddenly cold on his skin—sweep over him. His elbows suddenly clench against his ribs, and he makes a sound as if he has been punched by Kael Grimes. He looks around quickly. The bald woman looks over at him with a kindly, concerned expression.

"Are you all right?"

"Yeah. Sorry," he mumbles.

"Are you sure?" she says. Her voice is soft, generous. "If you have any questions, let me know. I'm a nurse here."

David's gaze flickers to her head scarf, to her missing eyebrows.

"That is, I used to be," she says with wry smile. "Now I'm a patient."

"Sorry," David says. He doesn't know what to say beyond that, so he hunches his shoulders and pretends to read. After a suitable delay, when the nurse has returned to her study, he eases from the carrel and totes the book back to the shelf. He can't find its slot, so he jams it at random between two others; it's not like *Patterns of Hu-*

*man Malformation* is a best-seller that everybody's waiting
to check out. He lurks, out of sight, to make sure the
nurse is absorbed by her reading, then slinks past her and
Transparent Man to the door.

He hurries back to Cheetah's floor and arrives just as
she's coming out. She is wearing wide, black plastic
glasses, the cheapo kind optometrists give out after the
exam. He is not sure she can see him, so he waves. She
nods, then goes to the receptionist's desk to sign some papers. "Next stop, pharmacy, then we're out of here,"
Cheetah says when David joins her.

"We're gone," he answers. "We're already halfway
home."

Approaching the elevator, Cheetah pretends to be
blind—she bumps against the doorway and holds out a
hand as if to feel for the wall. David catches on immediately and guides her by an elbow. On any other occasion
this would be greatly amusing, but here people make
room for David and Cheetah, then don't look twice.
Here people have more important things on their minds.
Like dying.

8

That evening at the Trotwoods' house, David stays in his room.

"All you right, David?" Mrs. Trotwood calls through his door. "Can I get you anything? Bring you some supper?"

"I'm fine, thank you," he calls back. "Just have a lot of homework."

He lies on his bed staring at the ceiling. His room feels smaller, the overhead light brighter. Like an examination bulb. He turns it off and lies there.

Much later he puts on a bathrobe and goes downstairs. The Trotwoods' ground-floor bedroom door is ajar and a night-light on. He takes a breath and taps lightly on the doorframe.

"Hello? Is that you, David?" Margaret Trotwood says.

"Yes, ma'am. Just wanted to say good night." He has never done this before.

"Come in, son!" Earl Trotwood says. He turns on a small lamp and sits up in bed; he wears a nightcap, while

Mrs. Trotwood's full gray hair hangs loose on her shoulders.

"Is everything all right, David?" she asks.

"Yes. I've just been . . . thinking about things."

"What things, David?" She pauses. "You mean, like girls?"

"For heaven's sake, Margaret," Mr. Trotwood says; the blanket twitches as he nudges her leg under the covers.

"Well, actually I do, sort of, have a girlfriend—but not to worry, we're just friends."

"That's good to hear, David," Earl Trotwood says. He gives him a wink.

"I was wondering if I could use the office tonight. I'd like to go online and look up some things."

"You won't look at pornography, will you?" Mrs. Trotwood asks.

"For heaven's sake, Margaret!" her husband says; he nudges her again with his foot.

"I won't, I promise," David says.

"You see," Margaret says to Earl. "It never hurts to ask."

David closes the door and crosses the yard, silvery in the moonlight, to the nearest gleaming barn. Behind him on the wide lawn, the Trotwoods' house sits erect and pale and tall, with dark windows and a shadowy front porch. So much space, so much silence here in the Midwest—he'll never get used to it.

Unlocking the door with Mr. Trotwood's key, he smells medicines, minerals, and hogs. Multiple wall monitors—six screens—carry live, black-and-white video feeds of the hog pens. The interior barn lights, on timers, are dimmed slightly at night, and the hogs in their endless metal pens sleep like walruses. Like seals. Some of the sows twitch and shift and flop—what do hogs dream of?—then lie motionless again and let out long hog breaths that rattle their noses and floppy lips. David turns up the volume on one monitor. At low decibels, the sound of a thousand hogs snoring is like the ocean, like the unending wash of waves on gravel and sand.

But he is not here to look at hogs. David goes online. He Googles Beth Israel, finds the hospital's home page, scrolls through it. Nothing interesting. He returns to Google and types in the name of his condition. With a few clicks he finds a medical-text search engine that takes him straight to Doctors Akbar, Ramaswamy, and Wisman. To their Beth Israel studies.

Too easy, really.

And too fast. There is, of course, the disclaimer ("Warning: The following article is intended for medical professionals and should not be used for diagnosis or treatment in lieu of board-certified medical counsel and treatment"), and suddenly, surrounded by written text ("vascularity . . . dermis redundancy . . . avian dactylicism"), there is little Charles LaBattier, age two.

The boy lies on an examining table. He is framed on all sides by meter sticks for measuring purposes. His arms are held outstretched by white-sleeved and rubber-gloved doctors' hands—this to extend the wrinkly flaps of skin beneath his armpits. *Dermis redundancy.* He looks like a little bird. A bat. A butterfly pinned in a glass case. His mouth is open, and he is soundlessly wailing.

David hears himself mouth-breathing. With a rapid keystroke he quits the screen, then stumbles up from Mr. Trotwood's desk. Hurriedly he locks the office door behind him and heads across the yard, walking faster and faster toward the house. Once safely back in his room, he lies in bed, waiting a long time for sleep.

*Jo-Jo and T-Boy are chasing him. His mother has left him alone for a few minutes while she goes to the market for bagels. While playing on the stoop of his apartment building, he is ambushed by these two neighborhood mini-thugs. Both go to his elementary school; both, like him, are six years old, in first grade.*

*"Hey, Ugly Boy, where's your momma now!" they shout as they rush him. He is cut off from his doorway and can only think to run. They chase him down the street, just around the corner from St. Mark's Church. "Ugly Boy, Ugly Boy!" they chant.*

*A produce truck is backed up on the sidewalk, blocking the street—suddenly he is cornered. His only escape is* down an alley and up the iron rungs of a partly lowered fire escape ladder clinging to the façade of an abandoned apartment building. They scramble after him, but he quickly outdistances them. He is a great climber. Soon he's several floors above them; Jo-Jo and T-Boy come up two stories at most, then stop.

"Hey, up here, guys!" he calls. Nobody climbs better than he does.

They look below to the alley, then up at him.

"What's the matter, scared?" he shouts.

"Shut up!" Jo-Jo shouts back.

"Aren't you coming? It's great up here!"

"We'll get you someday, you freak!" T-Boy calls.

He sticks out his tongue and makes weird flapping gestures. Then, in a victorious frenzy, he unzips his fly and pees on them.

In the warm yellow rain, Jo-Jo and T-Boy scream with rage and scramble to the ground. They stamp and swear. They pitch rocks at him, but their missiles fall short. He continues to taunt them from above.

They whisper to each other, then look back up at him. "Okay, Charles, you win," Jo-Jo says, and they walk dejectedly away. There is something false in their postures, but he is too full of victory to notice. He stands there, King of the Alleyways, Prince of Fire Escapes, and flings his arms skyward.

Soon, however, he takes stock of his situation. His T-shirt

*is badly torn, plus it's getting dark in the alley. Jo-Jo and T-Boy will be waiting for him somewhere below. His mother will be frantic. He sits there, weighing his options.*

*Suddenly there is scuffling, then clanging just above him. Jo-Jo and T-Boy lean out a vacant window. They carry sticks and pieces of brick. "Now where you gonna go, Freaky Boy?" Jo-Jo crows.*

*He shrieks—and jumps.*

*There is no thought of consequences. Instinctively he stretches out his arms—and feels his shirt rip apart, his skin ripple, a tearing sensation in his armpits. Like hook-and-pile ripping, like adhesions breaking loose—and then he is clumsily gliding, a plane without power, toward the far end of the alley.*

*He crashes into a pile of refuse and bounces like a thrown doll against a Dumpster. White daisies dance inside his head, but he staggers to his feet. He's alive!*

*He looks down at his arms. At the baggy flesh in his armpits already contracting inside his torn T-shirt. Then he stares up at Jo-Jo and T-Boy. Their necks are outstretched like those of birds, their jaws are slack, their mouths hang open. They look like gargoyles on the Chrysler Building. Then both shriek and disappear from the window like rats back into a wall.*

*He limps home. His mother is beside herself with worry.*

*"What happened to you!" she wails.*

*"I fell," he lies. Sort of.*

*She knows he has been chased and tormented again. She*

*holds him and begins to weep, but for the first time he*
*pushes her. Pushes away his own mother.*

He wakes up sweating. Someone is tapping on his bedroom door.

"David? Are you all right?" It's Mrs. Trotwood.

"Ahhh . . . yes," he calls.

"You were having a nightmare," she says. "We could
hear all the way downstairs."

"I'm very sorry," he mumbles. "I'm okay now."

In the morning, David makes a point of normalcy. All the usual words with Mrs. Trotwood, all the same movements about the kitchen, all the same timing out the door.

"Have a good day at school," Mrs. Trotwood calls. "And don't forget your lunch!"

He has indeed forgotten his lunch. He comes back into the kitchen. "Thanks," he says, and gives her the briefest of hugs.

"David!" she says, surprised, but he escapes her clutches and is off.

At school he arrives right on time and gets out of his pickup—to be slammed onto its hood. For a millisecond he thinks a tree has fallen on him, but then his arm is wrenched tighter than a chicken's wing.

"Hey, Fly-boy, we want to know how you did it." The breath is rank with chewing tobacco and Mountain Dew: Kael Grimes. Kael and his band of thugs.

"Did what?" David groans.

"Flew off Barn Bluff."

"What are you talking about?"

"You know exactly what I'm talking about. Flew off that night you were gonna get your beating, then flew off again when your buddy Max and his girlfriend saw you."

"Max who?"

"Max who used to go to Valley View—just like you, loser." David's arm is wrenched higher. "Your pal has been talking up a storm."

"Okay, okay. I . . . had these ropes stashed."

"No you didn't," Kael says.

"Sure I did. This rope ladder—*oww!*"

Kael hikes David's arm still higher; pain pierces through David's shoulder all the way into his brain. "Word gets around, right? Your pal Max and me got to comparing stories. And you know what? We think you're weirder than anyone ever thought. In fact, I think you're the weirdest kid in the freaking world, and I'm gonna make sure everybody knows."

Tires squeal on asphalt; a horn beeps and continues beeping. "What the—?" Kael says.

"Watch out!" someone shouts, and suddenly David's arm is released. Kael leaps aside as Cheetah's Toyota skids to a stop within inches of him; her car door slams.

"What are you doing to him!" Cheetah storms up to Kael like a cat with its ruff up, like a bird defending its nest. "You and your bunch of losers get out of here—right now!" she shouts. Clevie James comes rushing up and lays a stream of gangsta threats on Kael that could scorch auto paint; Kael retreats, walking backward, to his truck. His pals are already inside.

"I'm onto you, Fly-boy," shouts Kael. "Big-time! I know where you live, too. You can't hide on no hog farm."

Kael departs in a rattle of loose gravel.

"Who's that ugly dude?" Clevie asks.

"Yeah? What was that all about?" Cheetah says.

David straightens, stretches his back to one side and then the other to make sure everything works. "Just a friend. From back in the day."

"Some friend," Clevie says. He cocks his head, strokes his little goatee. "David, dude, we worry about you, man. You got more 'back in the day' shit than all of us put together. What's the deal, anyway?"

David pauses. Leans down to Clevie. "I'm in a witness protection program," he whispers. "Russian mobsters."

Clevie's eyes go wide—then he cracks up and goes away laughing.

That day in the hallways and at lunch, neither Max nor Janet will look David in the eye, but other students make up for it with all their staring. There are murmurs, whispers as he passes. The giant toilet has flushed again; he feels his life whirling, spinning, a vortex pulling him down.

He cuts out early and drives home. The highway curves around several bluffs, passes calendar-pretty river bends, then rises to flat and open farmland. When he first moved here from Minneapolis, the enormous open space of the countryside was frightening. Riding in the backseat of the Trotwoods' car, he often closed his eyes coming and going.

But now he is used the countryside (plus it helps to drive with one's eyes open). Today farmers drive their big machines in the fields, planting corn and soybeans. Twice, men inside tractor cabs with tinted windows wave briefly at him (at the Trotwoods' pickup, actually) as they make their turns at field's end. David returns the wave. It is a pleasing exchange—a passing "Hello" with no conversation or close inspection required.

He drives on, nearly "home" now. There would be room for someone like him somewhere deeper in the Midwest. Say, the Dakotas. A farm, a ranch somewhere. As long as he could drive a tractor (which he cannot, but Mr. Trotwood would show him), he could catch on, get a job. Mrs. Trotwood has told him of some of the hired men they have had over the years, "odds and sods" she called them. Alcoholics. Loners. Angry men. Sad men. Men with histories. Men with secrets. Men who preferred to be paid in cash, and always, some morning, were gone.

Like he might have to be soon.

He turns up the long, graveled driveway. Ahead is the Trotwoods' big white farmhouse with the wide front porch. The spreading oak tree in the front yard. The willow by the machine shed with the faintest hint of yellow in its weeping branches. If he disappeared, if he ran away, he wonders whether the Trotwoods would miss him more or less than some of their other "kids." How soon would they find a replacement? Several months? Several weeks? The next day?

Mrs. Trotwood, hearing his truck, comes onto the porch in her apron and waves to him. Living here, he sometimes feels as if he should have a handsome collie named Shep. He toots the horn.

"Fresh cinnamon rolls, David," she calls. "Piping hot!"

"Coming!" he calls. Inside the kitchen, the cooking smells catapult him back to the bakeries on the Lower East Side, the smell of Jewish rye and bagels. He closes his eyes, takes in the scent. He wonders if he is going crazy.

"How was your day?" Mrs. Trotwood asks cheerfully as she sets out the butter and a tall glass of milk.

He is silent. Usually he gives her a deceitful "Great" that today he cannot muster. He drops his book bag heavily on the stairs and takes his place at the counter.

"Any trouble, David?" she says with genuine concern.

He has that same sensation he has with Cheetah—he wants to tell Mrs. Trotwood things, everything, just blurt it all out.

"Mrs. Trotwood, has anyone inquired about me recently?"

She looks puzzled. "How do you mean, David?"

"I mean, like, where I came from? Who my mother was? Where I grew up?"

"Well no, nothing like that," she answers.

"But other things?"

She swallows. "People are always . . . curious," she says, beginning to color and bustle now, the willies setting in.

"About what?" he presses.

"Nothing," she says too quickly.

"About what's wrong with me?"

"We are all God's creatures, David," she says firmly.

"That's for sure," he mutters.

She looks at him, then down at her hands—then back up to David. "Look at me," she says. "There's no plainer-looking farm wife in the whole Midwest. I have a face like a potato, shoulders like an old workhorse. Don't you think I'd like to be beautiful, like Elizabeth Taylor? Sure I would. But that's not going to happen. No matter how we look, we are all God's children."

"God," David says hoarsely. "*God?*" His voice is so angry and strangled that Mrs. Trotwood thinks he is cursing. That he has gone mad. She stumbles backward and holds up her rolling pin as if to defend herself. David's mouth falls open at that—and then, weirdly, he begins to cry. He sits down, drops his head to his arms, and cries like a baby. "I'm so sorry."

"No, I'm sorry, David. You just sort of . . . scared me." She comes up behind and hugs him. He pulls away quickly.

"Oh dear," she says, flustered. "I know you don't like to be hugged."

"It's okay. And I didn't mean to shout. I don't know what came over me," he says.

"Just a bad day, I'd guess," she says, busy now, her back to him, her cheerful voice returning.

"Well, I'd best get changed, ma'am. I have the lawn mowing to do."

"And don't forget the potatoes in the garden," she adds brightly, as if nothing has passed between them.

He goes up to his room. If he squints, the narrow stairway is from an apartment building in his past. He closes his eyes and widens his nostrils; he searches for the smells of people behind doors, beyond walls—the odors of garlic or curry—and his mother's scent, woodlike, like planed and seasoned boards, steady and reassuring. But when he opens the door to his little room, there is no one home.

David likes operating the riding lawn mower, a sturdy John Deere with twin blades and a cutting swath over three feet wide. The lawn is huge here, almost three acres, enough for a soccer field and then some. It reminds him a little of Central Park. The garden is at the far side, close to a small stream from which Mr. Trotwood pumps water (softer and with less iron content than well water) for the vegetables, two long rows of potatoes so far, and the spring tulips rising like a tiny green sharp-pointed fence.

David ensures that his "hearing aids" are secure, checks

the oil and gas, then starts up the mower. It is not unlike a tractor, and driving it gives him great pleasure. He takes pride in the lawn, in its perfect green dimensions, and he sits straight astride the mower as it hums along. Slowly, gradually, he feels the threat of Kael Grimes begin to fade, sloughing off like dead skin. Nothing can touch him here. The mower is his hovercraft, a helicopter lifting him just off the ground, carrying him along on a magic carpet of air and green wet-plush fiber.

Near the garden, in thicker, damper grass, the wash of air from the spinning blades kicks up a flutter of small cabbage butterflies. His right hand, with an instinct of its own, snakes upward from the steering wheel and catches one; at the same moment a motion to the side catches his eye—freezes his arm in midair. It is Mr. Trotwood, passing from the nearest barn to the house. He waves. David stiffens in his seat and waves again, for real this time, an awkward, raised-fist, mower-power salute. Mr. Trotwood is pleased; he nods at David's good work and passes on. David lets out a breath. When Earl is safely in the house, David glances around, then slips the cabbage white into his mouth. It has the flavor of a communion wafer: neutral, unobjectionable. He drives on, leaving a fragrant contrail of green clippings behind, nipping off only the stupidest and slowest of the white butterflies, until suppertime.

During the meal (pot roast and gravy), Earl Trotwood brings up the matter of bullies in town and strangers who might want to "bother" David (clearly Margaret has been talking). "I just want you know that you're safe here, David," he says.

"Thank you, sir," he says. And his voice breaks. "I'd better finish my other chores," he says, and hurries up from the table.

"But your dessert?" Mrs. Trotwood says.

"Margaret," Earl says sternly, and David is out the door.

It is also David's job to hoe the potatoes. He takes a long-handled, sharp-bladed garden hoe and goes to work. Potatoes are important to the Trotwoods, and their care is the least he can do for them. He slices away weeds and hills up dirt about the dusky green plants, which are coming along nicely; each is about eight inches tall with spreading leaves above the lumpy black earth below, where the tubers grow. He does not mind hoeing; it is routine and regular, like mowing, and he falls into its rhythm.

Slice, pull, tamp.

Slice, pull, tamp.

Slice, pull, tamp.

Then, as the hoe's blade brushes against a plant, a plump beetle falls onto the dirt. He kneels down to examine it. It is yellow with black stripes, has six legs, and is as fat as a raisin: a Colorado potato beetle. He glances around. The Trotwoods are both inside the house. He pops it into his mouth. It is pleasantly bitter, like a dark Irish beer (when he was a child, his mother gave him sips of everything she drank), with a nose of marigold, a finish of hazelnut, and pleasing aftertastes of cabbage and carrot.

He stands up and continues his hoeing down the long row. Here and there, another beetle turns up, and he cannot resist them. The beetles increase in number toward the far, damper end of the garden, and as he makes his turn back up the second row, David continues to remove both weeds and beetles. Every garden should have such a worker; those master gardeners on television have nothing on him. He loses track of time (and potato bugs), until he hears sniffling.

He jerks upright, a particularly fat beetle pinched between two fingers. Near the garden's end, holding a plate and its wedge of shiny apple pie, is Mrs. Trotwood.

"Oh, Davy," she says, beginning to weep big-time, "it's not like I don't feed you."

10

He drives away in shame. He has to see Cheetah. Tell her — tell someone — everything.

Cheetah lives on the south side of Red Wing in a suburban cul-de-sac of older ramblers, 1960s vintage, that are on the edge of shabby. Her brick house is small behind its shrubs; Cheetah has the rear bedroom. David has been here once before, one day when Cheetah and he skipped school and had lunch together. After he parks, he slips around overgrown caragana shrubs and alongside the garage. A recycling bin is filled with empty wine bottles, the kind with green glass and screw-off caps. Staying low, he finds her window, takes a breath, and taps on the glass. Her room is dark (she sleeps at least twelve hours a day, sometimes more when she changes her meds). He taps again, louder this time. In the living room, he can hear a television show. Its laugh track.

Suddenly Cheetah's white face and raccoon eyes appear in the window. She squints and rubs her eyes. "David!" she mouths.

He puts a finger to his lips—motions for her to come out.

Soon enough she comes out the patio door and around to the side. "Are you all right?" she whispers.

He has no words.

"Come on, let's sit over there," she says. They go to the far, shadowy corner of the backyard, toward a battered teeter-totter and rusty swing set. "What's going on? What's happened?"

"I think I might be cracking up. Or something."

"Here, sit down," she says, motioning to the teeter-totter.

He takes one end, she the other.

"See, we balance each other," she says.

He manages a smile.

"I have this secret. Something about me," he blurts.

She waits. He shuffles his feet and rises suddenly into the air, which means that Cheetah drops. She laughs one quick, high note. Inside the house, the television goes mute; a little dog begins to yap. "Megan, are you all right out there?" her mother calls.

Megan. David brakes them to horizontal and looks over his shoulder for his escape route.

"Yes, Mom. Just getting some fresh air!" Cheetah calls.

There is silence, then television noise resumes, a comedy with loud laughter.

"So what's this 'thing,' this big bad secret?" Cheetah says as they resume their slow up-and-down motion.

He swallows; his throat closes up.

"Is it a boy kinda thing?" she asks coyly.

"As a matter of fact, yes," David says. "I have two penises."

"Wouldn't that be 'peni'?"

"I don't know—look it up," he says with annoyance.

This is stupid. He considers bolting from the teeter-totter, except that Cheetah would come down with a crash.

"Come on, David," she says softly, "you can tell me anything."

He is silent; they rise and fall a couple more times. "Actually, this a little beyond anything."

"Okay," she says. "Let me go first. How about my last big seizure? Doctors don't know what causes them. A tiny tumor, a hole in a blood vessel, something. Anyway, I'm sitting in the bakery downtown doing my homework when I start to feel strange. As in odd and different. Seizure people call this the 'aura.' Anyway, I start to get, like, warm all over. People around me turn different colors. Red, green, yellow, purple. Ghostly color doubles. Everything gets really loud. A coffee cup hitting a saucer is like a knifepoint in my eardrum. People's faces grow black freckles, and then cancer spots, spreading as I watch. The next thing I know, I'm lying on the floor with everybody staring down at me. And of course I've peed my pants again."

The teeter-totter by now is still. Balanced.

But Cheetah is not done. " 'Drugs,' someone says. 'She's overdosed on drugs. Call 911!' I want to tell them that my brain is naturally fried—that it produces too many electrons or something. I want to tell them that I don't smoke, I don't drink, I don't have sex or do any-thing most teenagers do because I'm always waiting for the next big one—which I know will come, just like earthquakes in California—but I can't say any of that be-cause my mouth is frozen open and I can't talk. So they cart me off to the ER, but as usual, I've come around by then and so it's all the more embarrassing. I go home and sleep for three days, and when I get up it's like I have to start my life all over again. From scratch. From zero."

David has his own kind of seizure. He lets her drop— abruptly, roughly—in the weedy sand and goes to her. She reaches for him, and he pulls her up, into his arms, and they kiss like crazy. His stocking cap comes off, and his weird ears are showing, but he doesn't care. She pulls him toward the bushes, and they are half walking, half stumbling, kissing like maniacs.

"Come to my room, David—you can slip in through the window," she breathes.

He keeps kissing her face, her neck as they stumble alongside the house; they cannot keep their hands off each other.

Then a patio screen door slides open and Cheetah's mother steps out. She is holding the little dog, about to let him down for his evening tinkle—when she sees Monster Man. Monster Man clutching her daughter. She drops the dog like a stone and screams.

||

Another close call for Phantom of the Opera. Jack the Ripper. Elephant Man. Creature from the Black Lagoon. David speeds away in his truck, his body trembling with desire more than fear, and he lets the Ford take him where it will. How far would Cheetah and he have gone? If she touched his secret skin, would she flinch? If she saw his naked body, would she scream?

He gets a grip. Drives slower. A great, heavy gloom descends inside his head. A black velvet curtain falling. A dark wall of storm clouds rolling in from the west. He can muster nothing against it. He finds himself driving in the old part of downtown Red Wing, along its low brick buildings, narrow streets, dark alleys. He passes abandoned diners and pharmacies, out-of-business department stores with façades stretching up to empty, high-ceilinged rooms. In New York City, they would have been converted to studios where artists painted or writers wrote or musicians played; here in the Midwest, no one's home.

His gloom, his anger worsens. He considers heading east, back to New York City. There, nobody cares about freaks. There, as at the Mayo Clinic, people have more important things on their minds. There's no time for staring. No time for anybody's business but your own. He checks his wallet: eight dollars and change.

The pickup takes him past the St. James Hotel and down to the riverfront by the railroad tracks. He parks by the old depot, closed and shuttered, and studies a stationary freight train, paused in the midst of its run through town. Several of the boxcars are dressed with graffiti: colorful, curving letters; shaded three-dimensional words; arrows, lines, and complicated gang symbols. Graffiti from far away.

He remembers subway cars rattling past with similar graffiti; thinks of the station at Second Avenue, of running with his mother to catch an uptown train.

Suddenly the boxcars jerk and clang. A chain reaction—*boom/boom/boom/boom*, car to car to car to car—followed, far down the track, by the lions-in-the-jungle growl of the diesel engines, then the tossed black manes of their smoke. Ever so slowly, the train begins to move. It picks up speed until it shudders out of sight around Barn Bluff.

Beside the empty railroad tracks, the bluff heaves up, dark and massive. His gaze climbs the rocky sides, the dusky, scrubby brush to the top, which still holds a blush of sunlight. The crown of trees glows. Something stirs in him. It is similar to the feeling when he is with Cheetah, though not a stirring in his crotch: more of a general agitation—as if blood or heat is moving from his head to his toes, out his arms to his fingertips and back again—an aura, his own kind of seizure. Dark thoughts recede. Vision sharpens. Sounds intensify. He feels his torso twitch—his arms instinctively tighten against his sides to hold back the sensation. But he cannot.

Glancing over his shoulder, seeing only a jogger lost in her pounding rhythm, he slips along the river to the base of the bluff. Fifteen minutes later, panting, scrabbling, he is near the top. He has taken a path that is not a path—it is nearly vertical—but with perfectly placed roots and rocks to hold on to. He hardly remembers climbing (he thinks of the squirrels at Oak Leaf, how they leap through the crowns of the oak trees branch to branch without hesitation, without thought; how there must be some tiny squirrel brain in each paw, in each sharp claw).

In another minute he is just below the summit. He dislodges one "hearing aid" and cocks his head to listen (he was not careful enough last time he was here). Carefully he swivels his head side to side. There is only the whisper of grass. Mute, expectant stones. Hushed trees. He scrambles up the last few feet, then lies back, panting on the rocks.

As he catches his breath, he watches the afterglow of

sunset. A thin orange rind of color is squashed under a horizon of purple; he can still see the town below—and can possibly be seen, so he waits.

Listens.

When the blood stops thudding in his ears, he removes his earplugs. At first he tilts them away from his ears so as to let in only a trickle of sound; otherwise, it is painful. He has learned to go slowly—but still he flinches when the full river of the world's sound floods his ears.

Tonight he hears the train far off, halfway to Lake Pepin, clacking along at full speed, the tiny gaps between the iron rails crackling like snare drum staccatos. Closer in, an osprey screeches in the trees above the river bottoms. Far below him, a group of women emerge from the old St. James Hotel.

". . . and then I told I him if he cooked more, so would I—if you get what I mean."

"Well, did he?"

"No, not at all."

There is a spatter of laughter as bright as xylophone notes, then the women's voices are muffled as they get into a car: *thud, thud, thud-thud* go the doors.

Beside him, in the rocks, a small animal, a vole or a mouse, skitters like fingernails on a blackboard; mosquitoes, with a gathering whine like a hundred motocross bikes, pick up his scent and begin to home in on him.

It is dark now; dark enough. He stands up, peels off his sweatshirt, then ties it tightly around his waist. He flexes his arms. The lumpy crepes of flesh in his armpits and down his rib cage begin to tingle.

Release.

Unfold.

He imagines a moth emerging from its pupa, the damp wings as tightly folded as a Chinese fan. A dragonfly crawling free of its cast-off skin, beginning its milky stretching. He pulls off his T-shirt; the air is chilly on his torso, on his stretched, engorging skin. Below he can hear the river valley's night creatures coming alive: the great horned owl on its branch, breathing, listening; the rabbit somewhere below, twitching, nibbling at a blade of grass; a fox sniffing the river trail; a raccoon clattering a clamshell on the river rocks. Landward is the steady roar of Highway 61, its eighteen-wheelers downshifting, Jake-Braking on the long slopes. He hears everything as if it were broadcast through the world's highest fidelity stereo system: every note is razor sharp, a needle point to the skin, the tip of an icicle on his tongue. It is a grand symphony of sounds—but one suddenly cuts through all others.

*Click.*

*Click.*

*Click.*

It is the echolocation call of a brown bat.

He cocks his head to follow its flight—David cannot see the little bat, who is somewhere down over the river—but he follows its pulse, measures its frequency.

Because of his hearing "problem," David has studied the elements of sound. There is constant-frequency sound, and there is frequency-modulated sound. Bats use both in their clucking, clicking calls, and at levels above the frequencies that humans can hear. Some bats are "whisperers," others have *thump-thump-thumping* calls. Tonight Mr. Brown Bat flies along, pitching forward a single, continuous pulse in a narrow band of frequencies. Cruising, and not for chicks. The little guy's bandwidth broadens. This is a bat in need of a mosquito, a mayfly, a cabbage butterfly. His call goes from *click-click-click* to *tickaticka-tickaticka* as he closes in. Then silence.

"Way to go, little dude," David murmurs.

He stands up on the cliff's edge. He extends his arms fully, shakes them as a diver loosens his shoulder and lat muscles. The drooping skin below them bells against the faint westerly breeze, cups the air. He can smell himself, the pungent odor from his armpits. When he is perfectly balanced, arms outstretched like the wings of an angel, he pitches himself into the night.

# 12

He flies no more than a parachutist or a flying squirrel flies. Like him, they mainly fall. No loops. No rolls. Not upward like an eagle, not backward like a hummingbird, just angling downward at a steady rate. As with a hang glider, the wind must be in David's face or he's in danger of dropping like a rock.

His flying is a lesser gift. If Rumpelstiltskin spun straw into gold, David spins hair, thin and stringy. If Jesus transformed water into wine, David turns it into root beer. A lesser gift, but it's his gift.

Night thermals wash over his face, over his bare arms, over his naked rib cage. Mosquitoes tickle his skin like windblown sand—he sucks in a couple—as he glides toward the dusky river bottom, toward a landing on the thick, soft grass of the shoreline.

Midflight he is suddenly surrounded by *click-click-clicka* and the darting shadows of bats. He laughs at the thought of his brothers-in-air puzzling at this swooping giant among them—this not-eagle, this not-owl, this not–flying elephant but a real, gliding boy.

He clucks his tongue back at them, which sends them into a frenzy of sound. Their clicks, as best he can guess, are on the order of "What the hell was that?"

He continues his descent, holding his head forward to counterbalance the weight of his legs, stretching his arms fully forward. The night air is perfect; the last heat of the day rises from the rocky bluff and provides a thermal lift—or maybe it's God's hand holding him up.

God letting him do this.

God giving him this one thing in return for his defects.

In a flash of insight that washes over him like warm air, David is filled with shame at his anger toward God. His rejection of Him. God, whose problems are way bigger than any human's. It occurs to David that God's greatest dilemma was His son, Jesus. The perfection of Jesus among imperfect humans made Jesus the Freak of Freaks, the Supreme Oddity. Jesus' gift of eternal life was, in human terms, the supreme defect!

Gliding on the soft spring night air, David understands this for the first time, and prays God will forgive his hard heart, his stupidity. He closes his eyes to cement the prayer, to send it forward—and when he opens them again he feels weightless.

Set free.

He banks to the right, a swooping turn, then to the left. He tries it again, a wider turn this time. Again it works!

These are maneuvers he has never tried, and for a moment he believes he really is flying. Then, in a steep left turn, he hits a pocket of cold air and drops like a stone.

He is close to the treetops, tall weeping willows, and he crashes into their branches. Flailing, whiplike branches. Time slows. Branches sharpen, thicken, solidify—thumping and punching him—*brack-bip-boomp-bonk*—as he tumbles groundward. The beating goes on. How many arms, how many hands, how many fists can one tree have?

# 13

David comes to by his truck. He is in the railroad depot parking lot. The tracks are empty. Red flashing lights stab at his eyes. Loud voices jab into his ears. His head hurts, there is something crusty on his face. He is surrounded by looming faces of paramedics. "Must have gotten mugged," one is saying.

"Drug deal gone bad," says another.

"Gangs," someone else offers, "right here in Red Wing."

David remembers the tree, its one final limb, how it whacked his forehead—the supernova of constellated light exploding behind his eyes. He remembers that he managed to put on his sweatshirt and insert his earplugs, then crawl to his truck—but he remembers this only in parts. The crusty stuff in his hair is leaking again.

"Maybe he's some runaway kid who fell out of a box-car," still another says as they strap him onto a gurney. "He don't look like he's from around here."

"Wait!" David mumbles. "I'm okay!"

"Hey, kid, you're alive!" one of the medics jokes.

"Yes. And really, I'm fine."

"What's your name, son?"

He pauses. "Gary. Gary Johnson."

"Well, Gary, you had a bad tumble of some kind. What happened?"

"Ah, I don't quite remember."

"He's concussed," somebody says.

"No, I assure you, I'm feeling much better. Great, in fact. I'd like to go home now."

"Gary, we'll have to let the doctor be the judge of that."

David struggles against the gurney's straps. "Where are you taking me?"

"To the emergency room at the hospital. We want to make sure there's no concussion, no broken bones."

"No, you can't!" he says. "You don't understand."

"Shhh. Just lie still. You're going to be fine," the nearest medic says. And, siren wailing, they head to the hospital. To the examining room.

On the way to the hospital, the medic takes out a cell phone. "We need to call your parents. However, they get less freaked if you do it. Are you able?"

David blinks. His parents? He thinks of his mother but then understands that the medics mean the Trotwoods. "Sure," he says.

He dials Cheetah's cell number. There is some clattering, fumbling, and then she answers, sleepily.

"Mom?" he says. "This is David."

The medic looks strangely at him; checks his clipboard.

"David Gary," he adds. "I've had this little accident—nothing serious, just a few bumps and scrapes. I'm wondering if you could meet me at the hospital emergency room?"

"David!" Cheetah whispers urgently. "What is going on?"

"Nothing serious, Mom. I just fell and scraped myself up a bit. But just as a precaution, they want to examine me."

"David!" Cheetah says. "Please tell me what the hell is happening! What's with David Gary?"

"Thanks, Mom," he says cheerfully. "See you at the hospital."

Cheetah arrives only minutes after him. He hears her voice, scared and loud, coming down the hallway. "I'm David's sister. Is he all right? Is he all right?"

"David? We have a Gary just arrived," the secretary says. "Gary Johnson?"

"Ah, that's him. I think. Gary is his middle name. David Gary Johnson. Sixteen or so? Tall, skinny?"

"That would be him."

Cheetah bursts into the room just as they are transferring him onto the crinkly paper of the examining table. The lights are terribly bright; Cheetah shields her eyes.

"David," she breathes. He blinks against the light, tries to wipe at the dried, caked stuff on his face, hair.

"Really, Sis, I'm fine," he says. "I was . . . climbing on the bluff and took a little tumble. That's all."

Cheetah has wild bed head. She looks around the room, and confusion gathers in her gray eyes. As the nurses begin to pull off his shoes, her gaze darts from the lights to the bright stainless-steel equipment to the scissors and clamps and the gauze pads and the blood pressure cuff to the faces of the nurses then back to the lights. As a nurse takes off his socks, Cheetah begins to blink rapidly and continuously.

"Cheetah," he says.

"Stay quiet. We need to get you out of those pants and that sweatshirt," a nurse says. The doctor bends over his face with a penlight.

But David is watching Cheetah, who has farther and farther-away eyes. She is starting to see things, things David can see, too: black spots, ghostly doubles, aurora borealis, cracks in the universe, wormholes in time. Her eyes cross as she follows her visions about the room. She reaches up both hands as if to touch something—to grab on to something. Then, like a shot duck on a cable television hunting show, Cheetah folds her wings and drops.

*Clock!* goes her head on the shiny white floor.

The emergency room physician glances over his shoulder. "Damn it!" he says. "Why do they let family in here, anyway?"

"Sorry, Doctor!" a nurse says, bending over Cheetah. "She sort of stormed her way in."

"Take care of her, people, all right?" the doctor says with annoyance. He begins to shine his penlight in David's eyes. He hears, at floor level, scuffling, then slapping sounds; the noise is like a large fish flopping on a wooden dock.

"Ah, Doctor?" a nurse says in an overly calm voice. "I think we have a seizure here."

The doctor swears for real this time. He looks at David. "Just lie quiet, son. I'll get back to you in a minute." As they all bend over Cheetah, David raises up on his elbows to look; they hold her down and try to put something in her mouth, some kind of rubber device to bite on; someone runs for another doctor, more help—a flurry of activity. Cheetah's body is electrified, surging with current, trembling, shuddering like a rocket tipped over on its launching pad, its engines roaring. Four adults can barely hold her, but David could: he wants to go to Cheetah, gather her in his arms. He swings his legs off the table, stands up drunkenly. Pausing to get his balance, he understands that no one is watching him: the doorway is clear.

He does not remember driving home.

He does remember the horrified look on Mrs. Trotwood's face as he comes into the kitchen. His stocking cap is gone, his ears in all their hugeness are fully exposed, and something warm still crawls on his scalp and down his neck.

"Earl, come quick!" Margaret cries. "David's had an accident!"

He does not fault the Trotwoods for taking him back to the hospital. He does not fault them for staying with him in the examining room, the same one as before. (Cheetah has her own hospital room by now; the seizure is over, but she remains under observation.)

"Please," he says weakly, as the nurses begin to peel off his sweatshirt. As in "Please don't." But he is dizzy and seeing his own Tweety Birds, and parrots and orchids and black dragonflies, and he knows the jig is up (what is the "jig" anyway? No one has ever explained "jig" to him). He smells his own musk and can only lie there as his torso is laid bare and shivering under the hot lights. He can only watch the faces staring down at him.

Watch the shock in their eyes.

The nurses gasp as one; they stumble backward.

The doctor grunts as if he has been punched in the gut. "What the hell do we have here?"

Margaret Trotwood sucks in a breath. Only Earl Trotwood does not flinch. His round, ruddy face and wide-set eyes remain unchanged, rock steady. "It's all right, David," he says. "We're here with you, son."

Earl Trotwood's steadiness at this moment probably has to do with farming in general and hogs in particular. Birth, death, all of nature's screwups in between—Earl has seen it. Among his thousands of little pink piglets

over the years, he has seen the runts, the two-headed, the
no-headed, the legless, the ones born inside out. Mistakes
happen in nature. There are errors. Defects. Earl Trotwood is undismayed by any of it. Nature is not perfect,
and so there is no reason to get worked up over that fact.

Drawing on his steadiness, Margaret Trotwood musters
herself. "You don't have to swear," she says. The doctor
looks up at her; he is more surprised at her complaint in
this, *his* examining room, than at the freak on his table.
"Excuse me?" he says to her.

"I said there's no reason to swear—none at all." Her jaw
is set, her face flushed. "This here is our son you're talking about." She steps forward to put her hand on David's
bare shoulder. He clutches her thick, warm fingers. Earl
Trotwood joins his wife close by. They glare at the doctor—dare him to say anything more.

"Dad. Mom," David says weakly.

And then the room spins, tilts.

Goes white.

# 14

He wakes up in a hospital room with Cheetah sitting by his bed. He has a concussion, six stitches above his left ear, and two cracked ribs; she has several stitches in the back of her scalp.

"Welcome to Headache Acres," she says. He blinks and looks at her. It is early morning; the sun is just coming up. He can hear nurses down the hall, beeping sounds, and the occasional groan from a patient.

"So what happened to you, anyway?" Cheetah says.

"I was climbing on Barn Bluff and fell."

"What were you doing up there?"

"Teenagers. The stupid things they do."

A nurse comes to check his pupils by shining a small light in his eyes. "Good morning, David." The nurse is overly cheerful, as nurses are, and speaks loudly, as nurses do; however, she will not look him directly in the face. "During your exam last night the doctors noticed some . . . abnormality. Later this morning you'll be seeing a doctor from the Mayo Clinic. He wants to check on you," she says, and adjusts his blanket.

"Why?" David asks.

"Just to make sure everything's okay," she adds brightly. It's as if she's speaking to the bed. Conversing with the sheets.

"What kind of doctor?" he says.

"A . . . specialist," she says.

"What kind of a specialist?"

"A pediatric surgeon."

"I have a couple of cracked ribs and a concussion. Why do I need to see a surgeon?" But the nurse has already left the room.

As they wait for breakfast, David turns suddenly to Cheetah. "Your mother!"

Cheetah shrugs. "She thought I was being abducted."

"Great," David mutters.

"Actually, I told her you and I were in a theater production at school—that we were acting out this part."

He falls silent. "Were we?"

"No," Cheetah says. "Anyway, it was a lame excuse but the only one I could think of."

David looks away. "I suppose I do have a permanent costume."

Cheetah is silent for a while, then says, "You know, I do get tired of that."

"Tired of what?"

"You know what. So you're not Brad Pitt. I'm not freaking Gwyneth Paltrow."

"We have 'other' gifts, right?" he says.

"That's right." Cheetah's eyes get sleepy; she gets that drowsy, lovely, bedroom-eyes look again. "So what were you trying to tell me at my house last night? Your big secret."

He turns away again. "You don't want to know."

"Yes I do."

"Are you sure?"

"Positive."

"You won't be creeped out no matter what?"

"I won't be creeped out no matter what."

He takes a deep breath. "Well, the deal is . . ." He raises up on his elbows to look at her. She is waiting. Waiting with lovely, sleepy eyes.

"Just tell me," she murmurs.

"Well, the deal is, I have this sort of skin deformity."

"Let me guess: under those clothes you're covered in fish scales."

"No. I have wings."

She is silent for long moments. "Wings."

He nods.

"So show me."

"You're sure?"

"Yes."

He looks at her. Then he gets out of bed—winces and

steadies himself briefly until his head clears. Loosening his hospital gown, he lets the thin fabric slip to the floor; underneath the gown he is wearing boxers. He might be a freak of nature, but he is not a flasher.

"Ready?"

She nods.

He turns his back to her and raises his arms. He feels the tingling, the breaking loose, the hot ripping sensations as his secret flesh unfurls; he smells his sharp, animal scent releasing as the humid folds spread, like a peacock its fan, to their full, pink-veined skin-ness. There is screaming—a screech that goes on and on. He hunches over and scrambles into his gown.

"Go away!" Cheetah shouts. "Just go away!"

David whirls—and sees the nurse. The screaming nurse. She is standing in the doorway.

"Is that what they teach you—to frighten people?" Cheetah shouts at her. The nurse backpedals as if David is going to fly at her and peck her eyes out; she disappears through the door and slams it behind her. In the hallway, the breakfast tray clatters onto the floor, and glass breaks.

"Damn," David says, stumbling back into bed, yanking the sheet over his head. "I knew I shouldn't have!"

Cheetah is silent for a while. "Wow," she finally murmurs, "you really do."

He is afraid to meet her eyes.

"Look at me," Cheetah says.

He does.

"They're beautiful," Cheetah says. "Your wings. When I first met you, I knew you had secrets."

"Yeah, well, I used to have secrets," David says; he looks toward the door.

"You thought that was me screaming, didn't you?" Cheetah says.

"Sorry," David says. The side of his head is starting to hurt again.

"Hey, I've seen way weirder things during my seizures," Cheetah says.

"Thanks a lot," David grumbles.

"What I mean is, we both have wings. Mine are just inside my head."

They are quiet for a while.

"So that was you up on Barn Bluff—the guy Max and Janet saw—with the 'arm kites'?" Cheetah says suddenly.

David nods. "I go up there quite a lot. I thought I was alone that time."

"You need to stop doing stuff alone, David," Cheetah says softly. As she smiles, her eyes close, and she leans back in her chair.

He lies there, sheets drawn up to his chin, and begins to feel lighter and lighter. Like a feather. Like a cabbage butterfly. Weightless. Free. As happy as he's ever been. Which is scary.

# |5

In David's hospital room, he and Cheetah watch *Extreme Makeover* on ABC. Two contestants are chosen to "Go to L.A.!" A young African-American woman, mother of five kids, who has amazingly large ears. Rhubarb-leaf, foghorn-shaped, umbrellalike, supersize, extra-value ears. The other winner is a middle-aged white man whose nose looks like a potato, whose eyes are set no more than a thin pencil's width apart, and whose yellow teeth curl up like wood shavings from a carpenter's plane. God clearly whacked him with the Ugly Stick.

"Where did they find these people?" David says sarcastically.

"Stop that," Cheetah says without looking his way.

When the "You Have Been Chosen!" announcements are made, the woman screams with joy, dances wildly in place, then hugs her husband (who looks confused); she sweeps all her babies close to her, their backs to the camera, and continues to blubber onto their little round heads. The geeky guy, not used to hugging people (he lives with his parents), grins like a fool—which reveals even more bad teeth—and shakes hands with his mother and father. They clumsily hug one another and begin to praise the Lord.

"They're finally going to get their boy out of the house," says Cheetah.

"I knew you'd get into the swing of this show," David replies.

As they watch, he is aware of more noise and voices in the hospital hallway: it's evening, and the after-dinner visiting hours are in full swing. A male nurse pops his head in. "Either of you need anything?"

"Maybe some more ice water," David says.

"Sure." He leaves, and returns within a couple of minutes. Entering the room, he looks over his shoulder to the still-louder voices behind him.

"What's the deal?" David asks.

"What do you mean?"

"Out in the hallway."

"Busy tonight—really busy," the nurse says without meeting David's gaze.

On *Extreme Makeover* the two winners arrive in L.A. and are chauffeured through Westwood in a stretch limo to the offices of plastic surgeons. Each surgeon's face looks tighter (as Earl Trotwood might say) than a gnat's butt stretched over a rain barrel. Their teeth gleam like new piano keys. The woman bear-hugs her doctor, who is good at hugs (he is from California); the bucktoothed guy shakes hands awkwardly with his doctor. With black felt-tipped pens, the surgeons mark up their patients' faces. They draw $x$'s, loops, swirls, lines of dots, arrows—then lean back to admire their work: tribal, primitive facial art. Only when finished do they allow their patients to look into hand mirrors. Seeing herself, the woman weeps for joy and throws another hug; the ugly guy looks scared by all the lines and arrows. His surgeon gives him a big California hug; the geeky guy, after all, has the bigger operation, which involves moving a piece of bone from a rib and grafting it between his eyes. He'll also get rhinoplasty (nose job), along with tucks and pulls from top to bottom. The woman will get a chin implant; new "twins," as the surgeon calls them (breast implants); a tummy tuck; liposuction on her hips; and various dermatology procedures to smooth her skin. As his clinic's address in L.A. pops up on the screen, the surgeon says that these "remarkable ears" will be the biggest challenge of his career.

"No!" a loud voice says (it's the male nurse). "Unless you're family you can't go in there."

David and Cheetah turn to the doorway.

"I just want to see him," a woman says; for an instant she is halfway into the room, a strange woman with flat, dirty hair and a smudged coat, the kind of person who hangs around the public library all day muttering at the books, lecturing the lightbulbs. "I have a gift for him!"

"I'm sorry, no!" the male nurse says, and wrestles her

out of sight. A female nurse fills the doorway—stands with her arms crossed and back to David and Cheetah. David has a sinking, slipping, falling feeling.

"What was that all about?" Cheetah says.

"Beats me," David says quickly. He watches Cheetah, but her eyes refocus on *EM*. The surgeries, back and forth, proceed in collapsed time, followed by the requisite things-went-perfectly telephone calls to the families. The woman's husband has gotten with the program; he sounds more full of joy than a televangelist. The geeky guy's parents sound drunk. *EM* slides through eight weeks of recovery, spa treatments, and power shopping in L.A., then culminates, back home, in "the reveal."

The families of both winners gather in grand hotels, and their extremely made-over loved ones make their grand entrances—as if arriving at a masked ball or at least a Mardi Gras party. At the moment of "reveal," there are gasps, shrieks, wild shimmying (the black family), and actual hugs in the white family. The formerly geeky guy now looks a lot like Mel Gibson; the woman looks remarkably like Whitney Houston. She is wearing a sparkling, low-cut, spaghetti-strap dress, and her husband's eyes are not on her perfect ears. "My babies," she shrieks. Her children, three little girls and two little boys, rush her. They look up at their mother with wet, dark eyes filled with love and fear. Each of them has giant rhubarb-leaf, supersize ears.

Back at the ranch, Mel Gibson's parents are definitely

in their cups. Mel's ugly brother (not ugly enough to be a winner) looks on gamely at the two foxy-looking women hanging on to Mel. The women, who themselves have had major work done, are allegedly cheerleaders from high school days; they've come to make amends for teasing Mr. Geek.

"We were *so* cruel to Jerry!" says one.

"I've *always* felt terrible about it!" says the other.

"Yeah, right!" Cheetah mutters at them.

"Great show, yes?" David says.

"It's totally sick!" Cheetah says. "Like, what do they all do *after* the makeover—when they're this totally new person? That's what I'd like to know."

"I'd say Jerry gets the girls, and the other woman dumps her husband."

In the middle of *EM*'s happy ending, the male nurse comes in. Using his overly cheerful, this-is-all-routine voice, he says to David, "Just a heads-up: a bit later we'll be moving you to a different room."

"Say what?"

The nurse repeats himself. David mutes the television. "Why?"

The nurse pauses to look directly at David, then lowers his voice. "In truth, we have sort of a . . . security problem."

David glances to the doorway, toward the voices growing louder, the buzz in the hall.

"That woman who was just here?" the nurse says apologetically. "We have, well, too many . . . unknown people who want to talk to you."

"Why would they want to talk to me?" David says, narrowing his eyes; he wants the nurse to say the words.

"I'm sure I don't know," the nurse says, his face coloring slightly; he averts his eyes as he straightens David's blankets. "Ring if you need anything."

When he leaves, latching the door solidly behind him, David turns to Cheetah. "I've got to get out of here," he whispers.

"How?" Cheetah says. She still looks very pale.

David glances at the door; he turns his head sideways and dislodges an earplug. He listens. "There's somebody standing just outside the door. Like a guard or something."

Cheetah watches David, not the door. "So those are not really hearing aids."

David shrugs. "Not really."

"They're just the opposite."

David nods.

"And your wings. I wasn't dreaming."

David is silent.

"Wow," Cheetah says. She leans back and stares at the ceiling for long moments. "Maybe you really do have two penises."

"No—that was a stupid joke."

"Are you sure?"

"Yes!" says David, exasperated.

She is teasing, of course. She lowers her voice to a husky whisper. "I know how you could prove it to me."

David's eyes widen.

"Not at the moment, of course," Cheetah says. "But someday soon, I hope."

"Whoa," David says. "Are you saying—"

"Yes."

David gets out of bed, crosses the pale linoleum to her chair, and kisses her. She pulls him close. "But you're right. You have to go," she whispers. "I can throw a fit, have a seizure or something, and you can slip out. Like last time."

David hugs her once more, hard, then steps away. "Actually, there's an easier way." He steps to the window. It's almost dark outside.

"What are you doing?" Cheetah whispers with alarm.

"What does it look like?" David says, leaning to look out the window. "It's only four stories."

"Still," Cheetah says.

"Don't you want to see?"

"No. I don't know. Maybe. As long as you don't kill yourself."

"No chance." Which is technically not true. But first he must deal with the window. Luckily this is an old hospital, with windows that used to open. Now a narrow metal bar screwed onto the sill keeps the tall glass rectangle from sliding sideways.

"You wouldn't happen to have a screwdriver?"

"Yeah, right. I always carry one," Cheetah answers.

David thinks a moment. Looks about the room. In the bedside table's top drawer are some basic medical supplies: tape, gauze packages, blunt-nosed scissors.

"Got it covered," he says, grabbing the scissors. Between pieces of the metal framing of his bed he inserts the scissor blades and, squinting, bends them until they snap. One of the narrow, sharp ends fits nicely into the screwhead. The screws, with some force, come out quickly, and the window, with the help of the metal pry bar, slides open.

David shrugs off his hospital gown, slips into his jeans and tennis shoes, then ties his crusty hooded sweatshirt around his waist. His skinny torso. He can feel Cheetah's eyes on him.

"Looking good," she says, but there is fear in her voice.

"Yeah, right." He cocks his head again toward the hallway, then unlatches the window. Below, the night street is empty but for a few parked cars and the fuzzy glow of streetlights. Cheetah comes to his side.

"Are you sure?" she asks; she looks down to the parking lot below.

"Hey, no big deal—I swear," he says.

"When will I see you?"

"Soon. Don't worry." He gives her a quick kiss.

She seems to be trying not to cry.

Through the window, fresh, cool air washes into the room. "This won't be my best stuff," David says. "Next time I'll show you the real thing."

Cheetah nods, but there are tears in her eyes. "Be careful, David!"

He faces the open window, its swell of air, and closes his eyes. Concentrates. Flexes his arms, feels the tearing, the brief burning along his ribs. Cheetah sucks in a breath as he hops onto the narrow sill. Crouched like a swimmer on his blocks, he counts to three—then pushes off.

David is gone. Like a parachutist on a base jump from a building or a bridge, he falls mostly straight down. As the ground punches up at him, his skin wings—at the last second—break his fall with a perfect grab, a swooping uplift. He lands on his feet, a stumbling touchdown on the narrow sidewalk. Immediately he turns to look back at the open window above. Cheetah is framed and backlit; she holds her hands over her mouth.

David waves to make it clear that he's okay, then blows her a kiss and pulls on his sweatshirt. What he does not notice, nor does Cheetah, is a teenager in a car with a video camera to his eye. When David and Cheetah are both out of sight, Max sits up to examine his footage. The tiny screen glows. There is a whoop of joy, after which he emerges from his car and does a stumbling, crazy, fist-pumping dance in the street.

# 16

The Trotwoods come with their car to the mouth of the alley. They were somewhere in the hospital, and David paged them, and told them where to meet him. They asked no questions.

"David?" Margaret Trotwood calls into the shadows. He emerges from alongside a brick building, hood pulled around his face, and slips into the car.

"Oh, David!" It's all she can say, over and over, as she hugs him. David lets her.

"Hush now," Earl Trotwood says. "Are you all right, son?"

David nods. He feels like crying. "Yes. Just a little headache, that's all."

"The hospital waiting room. It's a zoo, all those crazy people!" Margaret Trotwood blurts. "They have gifts for . . . they want to see you . . . they—"

"That's enough, Margaret," Earl says. "We need to get

home, then figure out what's next." He accelerates away with a chirp of tire rubber.

David sleeps that night like a hibernating squirrel: one ear open for predators, the rest of him deep under the leaves of his blankets. He is aware of Margaret Trotwood coming and going from his room, sometimes sitting in a chair while he sleeps, but he doesn't mind. He also hears the phone ringing, first one call, then another and another; at one point Earl Trotwood swears at someone, something clatters, and after that there are no more calls.

In the morning, Margaret brings him breakfast in bed. "I should have been a nurse," she says brightly.

"You'd be great," David says, and eats rapidly; he can't get enough pancakes. Earl Trotwood comes upstairs and joins them in David's tiny room.

"How's your head, son?" he says.

"Better. Hardly any headache today."

Earl parts David's hair, looks at his stitches. "Looks fine, though they're better at stitches than at barbering."

"David's hair will grow back," Margaret says, bustling about, unable to keep from tidying his room.

"Open the shade if you like," David says. He feels some weird sense of freedom: he has no secrets anymore.

"No, let's not," she says—with a glance to Earl.

David stops eating; he looks at the window, then back.

Earl Trotwood clears his throat. "Those people—the nutty ones? They seem to have found out where we live."

"We do, too, David. I'm sure she's a fine person."

David is silent. He stares at the ceiling.

Earl Trotwood clears his throat. "We got a call from the hospital last night."

"They finally figured out I was gone?"

Earl nods.

"How long did it take?"

"A couple hours."

"And Cheetah?"

"She's okay."

David nods. "What else did the hospital want?"

"There's this doctor—a specialist—who's going to make a house call."

"Here?" David asks stupidly.

"Yes."

"Why?"

"To make sure you're okay. Then to . . . talk with you. It's that pediatric fellow from Mayo the hospital told you about."

David is silent.

"We've met him; he's a very nice man," Margaret says.

"You've met him?"

"We were talking with him last night when you paged us," Earl says.

David's eyes narrow.

"He just wanted some background before seeing you," Margaret adds quickly, "that's all."

David remains silent.

"He specializes in . . . cases like yours," Margaret says.

"Cases like mine."

Margaret flushes, then sets her jaw. "Yes. Children born with anything 'out of the ordinary,' as he put it."

"Well, that would be me," David says.

"Maybe if we met with him, at least he could help us figure out what to do next." Margaret looks to Earl, who nods encouragingly.

David is silent. He stares at the window shade for a long time. "Can I sleep on it for a while?"

"Sure, son, you do that."

"We'll be right downstairs," Margaret adds.

When David wakes, the window and its shade have gone dark. He stands up, peeks out; there are more cars now, and some sort of bonfire, around which a clot of people have gathered. Some hold candles. He can hear faint singing. Hymns of some kind. Downstairs, there is another voice in the house—a soft, lilting voice, a voice not from here: for an instant David is four years old and back with his mother in New York City.

"David? Are you up?" Margaret Trotwood calls. "There's someone here to see you."

# 17

"The Mayo doctor they told you about," Mrs. Trotwood calls.

David pauses near the bottom of the stairs, then steps forward into the living room, where the television flashes soundless news.

"This is Dr. . . ." Margaret Trotwood begins.

"Ramaswamy. Sidran Ramaswamy," the man says quickly. He stands up—a short, trim, lively man, with berry brown skin and a musical voice—his syllables as round and polished as pebbles in a stream. He smiles with kind, walnut-colored eyes. *The voice—those eyes— David sees a surgical mask, remembers those eyes just above the white band.* "Charles!" he says, clutching David's hand with both of his. "I'm so pleased to see you again—and right here under my nose all the time."

Earl and Margaret stare.

"His name was Charles then—back in New York City," Dr. Ramaswamy explains. "Charles LaBattier." He turns again to David. "I knew your birth mother, and I want to say how sorry I am."

"Sorry?" David says. The room tilts. Goes to freeze-frame.

Dr. Ramaswamy's gaze flickers to the Trotwoods, then back to David. "Oh dear, you don't know," he murmurs.

"Know what?" David's voice comes out pinched, strangled.

Dr. Ramaswamy puts his hand on David's arm, but David jerks it away.

"David, as you must have known, your mother struggled with addiction. Addiction to some very bad drugs."

David looks away.

"She was ill, with hepatitis C, even when you were a toddler."

David comes further unstuck in time. *The dark circles under her eyes . . . the naps they took together, when he would awaken but she wouldn't—him pulling on, jerking her arms, pulling her toes until she slowly roused herself. Sometimes he thought she was— But she always eventually woke up.*

"Oh, David," the Trotwoods say, and draw close. But he pulls away from them as well.

"Please, tell me. What about her?" he whispers to the doctor.

"She passed away last year. I'm very sorry."

David stares at the floor. At the hard nap of the gray and brown carpet; its tiny, hooked squares are a giant televi-

sion screen with digital breakup, a bad satellite feed—
which means this could all be wrong. *A bad movie. Someone else's dream.*

"When last year?" he hears himself say.

"Around Christmas, I believe."

He tries to pull meaning, some kind of pattern, from
the carpet, its grays and browns. *Like the color of her eyes,
the shades that always scared him.*

"As often happens, her cirrhosis turned to liver cancer."

"How do you know this?" David asks suddenly, angrily.

"My former colleagues contacted me," Dr. Ramaswamy says.

There is a pause.

"Why would they do that?" Margaret Trotwood asks.

Dr. Ramaswamy pauses. David feels the doctor's gaze.
"Because of David. They kept track of her because of
David."

"I don't understand," Earl Trotwood interjects.

"David is rather famous among doctors," Dr. Ramaswamy explains. "Famous among pediatric circles, I
mean to say. When your mother took you to your first
specialist? That was me—but you were too young to remember."

*A hospital from the outside, its tall gray sides; then in-
side, its long, loud hallways; the sharp, nose-itching smell
of medicines; the bright lights, the cold instruments of the
examining rooms; the doctor's muffled but singsong voice;*

*his mother always by his side, holding his hand tightly in hers.*

David speaks to the carpet. "There was a large machine with a swinging arm and a funnel-like eyeball," he says. "Its buzzing terrified me."

"That was my X-ray machine, David," Dr. Ramaswamy says quickly, "a dinosaur by today's standards. You had many X-rays, almost too many, I should think"—a shadow of a frown passes through his damp, brown eyes—"and many, many examinations."

*Cold measuring devices touching, pinching his secret skin.*

"The question was always about surgery," the doctor says, "a corrective operation. We argued about David."

"Please," Margaret Trotwood says, as if made dizzy by all this information. She motions to the couch in the living room. "I think we should all sit down."

"You're quite right, thank you," the doctor says. He waits politely until they are settled, then continues. "The medical issue, we all agreed, was vascularity in David's vestigial tissue. The venation was considerable even then, and quite complicated."

"His blood flow in . . . that area, you mean?" asks Earl Trotwood.

"Exactly," Dr. Ramaswamy answers. "The debate centered more on *when* than on how to do the operation. Should it be done early on to minimize reconstructive surgery and allow for the best natural healing as David grew? Or done later, when he had reached full growth, his blood vessels were mature in size, and microsurgery techniques had perhaps improved—which they have, I'm happy to say. But then you disappeared, David. I and my colleagues stayed in touch with your mother—begged her to tell us where you had gone, but she would never say."

"Good," David mutters.

"Of course, David. I understand," Dr. Ramaswamy says.

David is silent. His brain feels contracted. Shriveled. Shrunken. Or maybe it's his heart; he will never be the same after this moment. His mother gone. Passed away. Died. How could he not have felt anything—seen anything, some kind of sign—on the day she died?

"My enthusiasm for certain cases is sometimes to a fault," the doctor says, "and was especially back then. I was a new doctor—an ambitious young surgeon full of great dreams. I wanted to be a pioneer in my field, someone whose name rose to the very top. Heart surgeons have their Michael De Bakey, pediatric surgeons would have Sidran Ramaswamy. There were three of us—Akbar, Wisman, and myself—in practice together, and we were all looking for that breakthrough case, the one that would make our careers." Dr. Ramaswamy leans forward with nothing but honesty in his eyes. "And then, like a blessing from the gods, along comes young Charles La-Battier."

There is silence in the room but for the faint singing out by the road. Dr. Ramaswamy turns his head to the music; he frowns. "Perhaps now, however, the gods are mocking me."

"What do you mean?" Margaret Trotwood says.

"The three of us doctors had a pact. We agreed to share our research, our discoveries, our ideas. Though I was first to examine David, initially I did share my findings with my colleagues. Together we published a paper—"

" 'Aviate Dermis Redundancy,' " David says dully.

Dr. Ramaswamy's eyes widen like sunflowers in sunlight. "I'm honored, David. Deeply honored—and a little surprised!"

"There's nothing wrong with David's brain," Earl Trotwood says sharply.

"I always believed that as well," the doctor continues eagerly. "While you had some cephalic issues"—his hands rise instinctively to frame David's face—"I found no neurological problems. My colleagues were not so certain, and so we tested you endlessly. It was I, for example, who discovered that your hearing was not impaired."

The Trotwoods turn to David; their eyes go to his "hearing aids."

"They don't know?" Dr. Ramaswamy asks.

David slowly looks up to the Trotwoods.

"Oh dear," the doctor says. "Shall I tell them, David, or do you want to?"

David cannot speak. He has few words for anything.

"In a nutshell, David's hearing is off the charts—unexplainably good by any theory. He hears everything!"

"Everything?" Margaret Trotwood exclaims. Her face colors slightly, and she glances toward their bedroom door.

"Not everything," David says. "Sorry, I should have told you."

"Yes," Earl Trotwood says evenly. "You should have."

"Anyway, to my great shame, I did not share that information with my colleagues," the doctor continues. "Which was the beginning of a slippery slope. I put myself and my career first. I thought, After all, it was I who first examined Charles—David—so why shouldn't I get the credit?"

The Trotwoods are silent.

"To make a long story short, we began to argue over who would take credit for David and our research. We were unprofessional; we talked behind each other's backs and worse. Word got out about our feud, and our 'discovery.' Among pediatric surgeons, David was like a gold strike; there was a rush, a press of other doctors who wanted in on the action.

"David's mother did the only thing she could do. She pulled him out of treatment. When we persisted, she sent him away—he just disappeared—and none of us ever saw him again. From bitterness and mistrust, our practice broke up, and I moved west to the Mayo Clinic, where I've been ever since—so close to David all this time!"

"Well, doctors are only human," Margaret Trotwood murmurs.

"No," Dr. Ramaswamy replies firmly, "we should be better than that."

There is silence.

"Anyway," the doctor says to David, "the gods are both sly and wise, for here we are, together again."

"So now what?" David asks.

"Wait—" Margaret Trotwood says, her gaze beyond them on the cable news broadcast on television. She points.

They all turn and look at the television: LIVE FROM RED WING, MINNESOTA, the silent banner reads. On the screen, an attractive, black-haired woman reporter stands in front of the Red Wing hospital.

David's heart clenches like a fist.

Margaret Trotwood touches the remote; the sound comes on. "Reports coming in from this small midwestern town point toward a remarkable story—as of yet not fully confirmed. However, we have both medical and other witnesses who are speaking of what can only be described as, quote unquote, an 'injured angel.' "

"Oh dear," Margaret Trotwood says.

The reporter glances gravely at her notes. Dramatic pause. "Emergency medical technicians two nights ago discovered a disoriented, injured young male below the bluffs along the Mississippi River. Subsequent medical treatment revealed"—here the reporter clears her throat—

"revealed what appeared to be winglike appendages. I'm standing here with Mary Lou Anderson, a nurse on duty at the time. Mary Lou, what can you tell us?"

"Great," David says. The screaming nurse.

"I know I'm going to lose my job over this," the nurse says, starting to sob, "and I apologize to my family. But I saw them—the wings—there's no doubt about that. Ask the doctor, ask the other nurses!"

"Actually, we did," the reporter interrupts. "They wouldn't comment."

"Somebody has to tell the truth—somebody has to bear witness," Mary Lou blubbers. "God chose me, I guess. Praise Him!" She breaks down big-time.

The camera immediately draws tight onto the reporter's face. "We do have other witnesses, actual friends of this 'angel.' " She turns to Max from Oak Leaf, who blinks into the camera's lights as if he's been busted—and beside him, his girlfriend, Janet.

"I seen him fly!" Max blurts.

"Me, too," Janet says, leaning in to get her face on camera.

"Where, how have you seen this?" the reporter asks. "Be specific, please." She's not about to lose control of this interview.

"Up on Barn Bluff."

"The cliff along the river," the reporter clarifies.

"That's right. He goes up there and flies off. We've seen him."

By now Max and and Janet are getting into the fact that they're live on national television. "Hi, Mom," Janet mouths silently. Max grins and gives a longhorn salute to someone, and the camera cuts away immediately.

"Thank you," the reporter says. "Clearly questions remain, but the key one is this: Is there indeed an 'injured angel' in this small Minnesota community? And if so, why here, why now? Reporting live from Red Wing, I'm Sandra Cardenas."

Margaret turns the television off. It crackles and dies.

"Not good," Dr. Ramaswamy says.

Margaret Trotwood has set her jaw. "Who would believe those two kids? That's just plain crazy talk. What has happened to the news nowadays? You can't believe anything."

David looks down. Says nothing.

"But the nurse," Earl adds, as he stares at David.

"That nurse should be fired!" Margaret says; oddly, she begins to cry.

"I'm quite sure she will be," Dr. Ramaswamy answers.

"So now what?" Earl asks.

"I haven't a clue," Dr. Ramaswamy says. His voice is full of wonderment.

This strikes David as funny. He laughs loudly—a single note, more of a squawk than a laugh. They all look at him. He continues laughing in an unnaturally high voice, his guffaws coming louder and faster. The Trotwoods look at each other with concern. "It's all right," Dr.

Ramaswamy says softly, and puts his hand on David's head. David's laugh track plays faster and faster until he collapses sideways onto the couch, his chest heaving with unstoppable sobs. Mrs. Trotwood kneels beside him and holds his head to her breast. He does not pull away.

Afterward, the only thing to do is eat supper. Margaret Trotwood produces a major meal of pork chops (Dr. Ramaswamy leaves his untouched), mashed potatoes, green beans, bread rolls, and they talk about everything but David—until the doctor's brown eyes turn serious. "But you must tell us, David: is it true?"

"Is what true?" As if he didn't know.

"What the kids said on television."

There is silence around the table.

David looks apologetically to Margaret. "Generally, sort of, pretty much . . . yes."

Margaret Trotwood's face turns paler than snow. She stops eating.

"Good God, son," Earl says.

Or Bad God. But David thinks of those warm-air thermals rising up Barn Bluff, their hands softer than pillows, their arms stronger than blankets, and he tells them everything. The first time he flew away from the neighborhood bullies, Jo-Jo and T-Boy; how he continued his alley flights in the neighborhoods of NYC; how from medical bills they had to move again and again; how his mother sent him to distant relatives in Minneapolis; how she was supposed to follow him but never did.

"Did she know?" Margaret asks. "That you could . . . ?" She cannot say the word; she does not yet fully believe.

"I think so," David answers. "We never talked about it, and she never saw me in action. She probably didn't want to really—what mother would? I think she blamed herself."

"Your mother was a wonderful person," the doctor adds. "She had her hands full in many ways—had her own demons—but in the end she made the right decision for you."

"Yes," David says, and turns to the Trotwoods. "Yes she did."

The Trotwoods start to dab their eyes and honk their noses once again, and the mood lightens.

After dessert, Dr. Ramaswamy turns to David. "Would you mind terribly?"

David shrugs. "I thought you'd never ask," he says with no small trace of sarcasm.

"This won't take long," the doctor says quickly.

"Use our bedroom," Mrs. Trotwood says, "just the two of you." She cannot look at David.

David leads the way and sits on the edge of the Trotwoods' large bed. The doctor closes the door behind them.

Dr. Ramaswamy begins to hum softly as he opens his black briefcase. He takes out a palm-size tape recorder along with a stethoscope and some other measuring-type devices. First he looks at David's scalp wound, then shines his little penlight into his eyes, then into his ears. David flinches at his humming so close up. "Your ears! Sorry," Dr. Ramaswamy says quickly. With David's ear-plugs out, he speaks in whispers, which is just right for David.

"May I ask you to take off your shirt?" he asks.

David complies. His mind retreats to the neutral zone; he suspends himself in time and motion.

"And lift your arms, please?"

David obeys.

Dr. Ramaswamy begins to speak into his recorder in his native language, Hindi, David supposes, but maybe not; maybe it is some ancient tongue—Aramaic, Hebrew—because English cannot begin to explain what he sees.

"Could you lift them all the way?" the doctor asks. "As if you are . . ." He, too, does not use the word.

David closes his eyes. He concentrates: forces his secret skin to believe there is an open window, a valley below, a warm breeze. The tearing sensation, the stretching—like a thousand pinpricks—sends a ripple through his torso and down the muscles of his lower back: his pungent, woody odor floods the room. Dr. Ramaswamy emits a short exhalation—a grunt of joy—as if he has rounded a corner in a museum and come face-to-face with a famous painting or a sculpture. In David's case a Picasso or a Dalí. The doctor murmurs animatedly to himself. He tests and squeezes and pinches the underside of David's pink webbing, first with his fingers, then with a cold chrome caliper; he speaks into his recorder. He continues touching, kneading, measuring—first under one arm, then the other—then lowers David's hands.

"Enough," he says. "Thank you, David." He watches David's wings contract, draw together like fold-up fans, then helps him on with his shirt. They go back into the living room.

Earl Trotwood steps away from the side of the window, where he has been watching the watchers.

"Well?" Margaret Trotwood asks. "Is David . . . okay?"

"He's fine," the doctor says. "Top to bottom. I can see no medical reason to prevent him from having the corrective surgery. In fact, it would be a relatively simple operation."

The Trotwoods look to David.

"I also know a craniofacial surgeon who could give David a new look at the same time."

"You mean, remove his . . ." (Margaret cannot bring herself to say the word.) "And—"

"Fix his face, too, yes," the doctor says. "I'm quite sure it could all be in the same long day. His period of recovery would be about six weeks, give or take, with the facial healing taking the bulk of that time. His forehead, cheekbones, and chin"—the doctor's hands go to David's face and make a frame—"will require some osteopathy, primarily bone grafting, but nothing my colleague hasn't done many times over. In short, if we did the operations, within six weeks David could look like any other boy on the street—if not better."

There is silence in the living room; they all look at David.

Luckily (sort of), there is a loud knocking at the door. Earl swears under his breath and goes to answer it.

"Let's step out of sight, shall we, David?" Dr. Ramaswamy suggests.

David and the doctor retreat to the bedroom. It is the county sheriff at the door; David listens.

"Earl, I hate to bother you and your family, but we have a situation developing outside," the sheriff says.

"I see that," Earl says evenly. "We only ask that people not trespass."

"Fair enough," the sheriff says. "But have you looked lately?"

There is a rustling sound and footsteps as the two men go onto the porch. The singing loudens in the open doorway; Earl quickly pulls the door shut behind him. David dislodges one of his earplugs so as to hear through the wood.

The sheriff says, "I don't know quite what's going on here, but there's some pretty wild stories about . . ."

"Our son," Earl says. "David."

"Yes. Well, what I worry is that this is going to spin out of control—that we won't be able to hold them back. They just want to see him."

David goes to the window, flaps up his shade. Parked on the road are at least two dozen cars, a haphazard line of them along the fence that edges the property. They cannot come in the driveway because Earl Trotwood has parked his biggest tractor across it. Some of the people are slumped in their cars, others stand outside them; when David's shade goes up, there is a flurry of activity — car doors slam, people turn toward the house. Some raise binoculars to their eyes.

David sucks in a breath, yanks down the shade. He turns to the Trotwoods. "Now what?"

"We have no idea," Earl Trotwood says. Then, oddly, he begins to chuckle. Margaret and David stare at him, and soon they are all laughing as if they have just heard the all-time funniest Supreme Joke of Jokes.

"I'm sorry, son," Mr. Trotwood says, and then breaks up again.

"It's all right," David says, wiping his eyes.

"Really, Earl," Margaret says to her husband, which almost sets them off again.

The joke, of course, is on them; their laughter doesn't last long. David peeks again past the side of the shade.

"Crackpots," Earl says.

"Fanatics," Mrs. Trotwood says.

David lies back on his bed. Looks at the ceiling. "I think my mother always worried about this."

The Trotwoods are silent.

"I wish you could meet her."

"That's not going to happen," Earl says.

"I mean," the sheriff says, not listening, "it's like those crazy scenes down in Mexico or Brazil when somebody sees the face of Jesus in a tree trunk and thousands of people turn out to look."

"So what would you suggest we do?" Earl asks.

The sheriff scratches the beard stubble on his neck, making a sandpapery sound. "I'd say we have to get the kid out of here. The sooner the better."

# 18

Just before midnight, a medevac helicopter from Rochester descends onto the Trotwoods' front lawn. Emerging from the black, moonless sky, its landing lights probing downward like yellow legs and its single red eye flashing, the helicopter is an alien landing craft. The Mother Ship coming to retrieve its lost freak. David huddles with the sheriff and Dr. Ramaswamy by the front door until the chopper is on the ground. Deputies have set up a cordon to hold back the crowd, but there is a wailing—then a surge of people forward across the lawn.

"Damn," the sheriff mutters. "We're gonna have to make a run for it."

"I'm sorry there's no room for you," Dr. Ramaswamy says to the Trotwoods.

"We'll come by car tomorrow," Margaret says to David. "Trust Dr. Ramaswamy!"

David hugs his parents hard, then follows the sheriff

and Dr. Ramaswamy through the front door. At the sight of the sheriff, the doctor, and the hunched, hooded figure of David, women scream; men shout his name.

"David!"

"David—over here!"

Cameras flash.

"Michael Jackson's got nothing on you, kid," the sheriff says.

"Screw you," David says.

"Sorry—you know what I mean."

"No, I don't know what you mean!"

"Keep moving, son!" The sheriff hustles him along a gauntlet of camera flashes, looming faces, clutching hands.

"David! Over here, David!"

"Stand clear! Get back!" the sheriff shouts.

"David, please—look at me!"

"Me, David—touch me. See me!"

"David—take this! We made it for you!"

They thrust out posters, rough drawings, carvings, figures. They are all of angels: angels with two wings, angels with one wing, angels made of chicken feathers, angels made of cardboard, angels made of papier-mâché, angels made of yellow ear corn with white husk wings. Ahead, the helicopter's big rotor picks up speed; its landing struts become unsteady on the ground. The sheriff pushes David and Dr. Ramaswamy inside; hands buckle them in.

"Does anyone need immediate medical attention?" a technician shouts above the noise.

"No, just get us out of here," Dr. Ramaswamy says.

The helicopter pilot, with his helmet and radio headset, does not look back at David. Carefully he eases the chopper straight up, up and away; the throngs of people below shrink to black. Once clear of the bluffs, he banks south toward Rochester. "Well," Dr. Ramaswamy says, "that was fun!"

David does not reply. He prefers his way of flying— silent, fragrant air sliding over his bare skin like warm ocean swells, his arms outstretched and reaching—not strapped into a specimen jar with a thrash drummer pounding on the glass. He pulls his hood tighter around his head and turns his face to the glass. Below, the countryside slides along black except for the occasional tiny yellow finger of car lights. He worries about the Trotwoods, how they will cope. He worries about Cheetah—how will she find him? And the sad people left behind—where will they go, what will they do now?

A few blocks west of the Mayo Clinic, in a side wing of Saint Marys Hospital, David steps into his room. A suite actually. It has a king-size normal (not a hospital) bed, a Jacuzzi in the corner; a leather couch and big-screen television. He feels as if he's in a grand hotel, not a hospital. "We reserve space for special, often foreign visitors,"

Dr. Ramaswamy says. "You'll be quite comfortable and safe here."

Behind them, in the hallway, is a muscular guy in white gym shoes, tight T-shirt, and walkie-talkie on his belt; he nods slightly at David.

"Roy, your attendant, will be just outside if you have any questions or need anything at all."

"My 'attendant'?"

"He's there to assist you in any way. That includes making sure you aren't bothered by strangers."

David turns back to his room.

"There are toiletries, fresh clothes, books, magazines, newspapers—everything you need away from home," Dr. Ramaswamy says. Several of the magazines and newspapers are in a foreign script, and these the doctor sweeps into a drawer. "Unless you read Arabic?" he says with a smile.

"Sorry, no." Suddenly David is overwhelmingly, bone-achingly tired.

"I'll come by in the morning right after my rounds," the doctor says.

They shake hands, then David locks his door and falls into bed. He crashes hard, sliding into sleep like a train heading toward a dark tunnel, everything running and blinking faster and faster—then blackness.

In the morning he orders room service breakfast, which Roy delivers (he supposes someone is paying for this and

hopes it is not the Trotwoods), then flips through the
morning television channels. There is nothing about any
flying boy, which is good. Just the usual overly caffeinated
morning-show hosts finishing each other's sentences. He
dozes off again and awakens to the smiling face of Dr.
Ramaswamy.

"Good morning, David. You slept well?"

"Yes."

"I spoke to your parents last night and assured them
that you got here safely."

David nods, then looks around the suite. "Will they
have to pay for this?"

"Not to worry. The hospital has a fund for such things,"
the doctor replies.

"And Cheetah? My girlfriend?"

"The Trotwoods told me they have been in touch with
her."

David lets out a breath.

"We have much to do today," Dr. Ramaswamy says,
handing David a set of clean, hospital-type scrubs.

At 10:00 a.m., after passing through a maze of corridors,
hospital hallways, and "Restricted Areas," then riding a
short, private shuttle to a rear entrance to the Mayo
Clinic, they take the elevator up to the tenth floor. There
David meets Dr. Jenks, a craniofacial surgeon. A face
arranger. He is a tidy man with (of course) naturally perfect features, and his eyes meet David's only briefly; the

rest of the time their gaze moves about his face: side to side, top to bottom, then back again. Measuring, judging, evaluating—bone structure, cheekbones, eye sockets. Beside him is an attractive younger woman, probably a medical student or resident; Dr. Jenks does not introduce her.

"I'll leave the three of you to talk," Dr. Ramaswamy says to David.

"So," Dr. Jenks says—he makes an oval with his hands and frames David's face—"Dr. Ramaswamy thinks your face needs some work. What do *you* think, David?"

David shrugs. "I guess." His eyes go to the pretty young woman, but her gaze, like Dr. Jenks's, doesn't meet David's. To them his face is geometry. An equation. A proof to be solved.

"First we'll do some mapping," Dr. Jenks says. "My assistant will take some digital photographs, which we'll enter into our computer. They will give us precise facial measurements—for example, the width of the septum and the distance between your eyes. After that we'll do some computer imaging to see what we might do for you. And last, we'll need to do an MRI of your skull to check your coronal sutures."

"The stitches in my scalp?"

"No. By coronal sutures, I mean the bone plates that we all have in our heads. Babies have that soft spot— the fontanel—which eventually closes? Well, there are other, smaller, gaps between other bone plates, and sometimes in infancy they close prematurely, a condition called . . . ?" He turns to his assistant.

"Craniosynostosis," she finishes.

The doctor nods. "What I do is move some bone plates around just a bit, particularly in your forehead, orbital sockets, and jawline." With that, Dr. Jenks checks his watch and slides out the door.

"Not the warmest person in the world," the woman murmurs, "but a great surgeon."

David is silent.

She smiles. "My name is Sandra Smith. I'm completing my residency in facial reconstructive surgery with Dr. Jenks." She talks easily as she adjusts her tripod and camera, and then they are ready.

"Look straight at me, David."

He obeys.

"Turn sideways." Her hand is soft on his face as she positions it just so. She uses scented soap—lavender? peach? sandalwood? To his supreme embarrassment, he feels a stirring in his hospital pajamas. Thank God he is wearing a robe.

"*Beep, click; beep, click*" goes the camera.

"Thank you," Dr. Smith says. She attaches camera and USB cable to the computer, and after some rapid keystrokes, David's face flashes onto the oversize monitor. He looks away; any stirring anywhere in him vanishes at the same time.

Dr. Smith notices his reaction. "Hey, none of us think we take good pictures."

"Easy for you to say."

She pauses. "Why, thank you—I think."

David blushes.

Dr. Jenks reenters in the nick of time, reading a chart, which he tosses to Dr. Smith, then looks at David's face. His face on the monitor, that is.

"Grid, please," he says.

Dr. Smith is already on it; a black checkerboard of lines overlay themselves across David's face. Dr. Smith gives way to Dr. Jenks, who sits and begins to move the mouse to highlight different sections of David's face.

"This gives us your measurements," Dr. Smith says. David glances at her white lab coat buttoned snugly over her chest; he wishes she wouldn't use the word *measurements*.

"Good, good," murmurs Dr. Jenks to himself. He turns briefly to David. "For what we're about to do next—all on the computer, of course, and nothing to do with any real surgery—you are well-named."

"Michelangelo," Dr. Smith says. "His *David*."

"As a painter and sculptor, Michelangelo was particularly concerned with ideal forms—with perfection of the human body," Dr. Jenks continues.

"You mean, like Aristotle and the Greeks who preceded him," David says.

Dr. Jenks turns away from the screen to look at David,

then his assistant. He actually smiles. "As Dr. Rama-swamy said, there's nothing wrong with your brain."

"Maybe I could even be a doctor someday," David says.

Dr. Jenks pauses. He actually gets the sarcasm. "Anyway, we're not so much about perfection as Michelangelo, but we can certainly give you more balanced features."

David is silent.

"Would you like to see?" Dr. Jenks asks. He nods to Dr. Smith and hands her the mouse.

David shrugs. "All right." As if he has much choice.

Dr. Smith moves the mouse, and David's face begins to morph: his chin lengthens; his eyes draw closer; his forehead rises; his ears lift and shrink. In his real body, his stomach turns over; he hears himself breathing through his mouth.

"Are you all right?" Dr. Smith says. "This part can be a bit of a shock."

"I'm fine," David lies.

"Maybe a bit more chin," Dr. Jenks says to Dr. Smith. She obeys.

"I don't want to look like Jay Leno!" David says.

Dr. Smith laughs and takes a little off the chin. "How about Ben Affleck?" she says. "That would work for me."

For Dr. Jenks, this is a bit too much fun; his lips purse, and he makes a point of giving Dr. Smith further rapid instructions in high medical mumbo jumbo.

"Sorry, Doctor," she says, and continues to fine-tune David's face in silence.

"A bit more nose," Dr. Jenks says.

"Say when," Dr. Smith answers. She gives David's stubby nose length and strength.

"Ah . . . when?" David murmurs.

"No. A little more—there—very nice," Dr. Jenks says. "I like." He checks his watch. "My assistant will finish off this appointment and schedule your MRI. I will be in touch with Dr. Ramaswamy, who has the lead in all this. Today's visit was an introduction to what we do here— and what we can do for you. The final step, of course, is your decision."

David, having been brought up polite, puts out a hand, but Dr. Jenks has already turned away, speaking into a tape recorder as he departs.

"Like I said," Dr. Smith whispers, keeping her eyes on the screen.

The room suddenly has more space, more oxygen. "Really, David—what do you think?" she says as they look at the monitor.

David is silent. "It's a . . . little different."

"Psychologically it's a pretty big deal," she answers. "In fact, we require you to talk with one of our mental health counselors before any surgery is performed."

"A shrink? Why?"

"After substantial surgery, there can be complicated

identity issues. A small percentage of patients have difficulties over the long term."

"Identity issues? Like what?"

"Some patients experience a disconnect between who they feel like and who they now look like. Sort of like if you grew up as an obese child but became a trim, weight-proportionate adult—you might still carry the childhood self-image."

"The fat kid inside you," David says; he thinks of geeky Jerry from *Extreme Makeover,* Jerry who now looks like Mel Gibson—he wonders if he's had any luck with the ladies.

Dr. Smith nods. "Exactly."

David looks at the screen and shrugs. "I think I could deal with looking like that guy."

She pauses. Turns to him. "You wouldn't look like him, David, you'd *be* that guy."

19

Back in his room, David looks at the printout image of
New Guy.

New Guy Pinned on the Wall.

Dr. Smith made a big deal about his taking the image
along, looking at it often—all part of the "identification
process," she called it. She even printed him a wallet-size
photo.

"What say, bro?" David asks New Guy.

No answer. Not even a blink or a nod.

"Maybe we need a better name for you."

No answer.

"How about William?"

Nothing.

"Lance?"

Nothing.

"Pierre? Rafael? Encino Man?"

New Guy only stares.

"Not ready to talk yet? That's cool," David says. "Maybe if you had a body to go along with that head . . ."

*So what you got?*

"You're looking at it," David answers. He is standing and does a quick 360 for New Guy.

*That's it?*

"Read it and weep."

New Guy appears to mull that over. *Beggars can't be choosers, I guess. But I hear you're going to have some work done?*

"Maybe," David says.

*As in clip the wings?*

David shrugs. "Thinking about it."

*We'd be cool with that.*

"Hey—speak for yourself."

*Sorry. I'd be cool with that.*

"That's more like it."

*But what about afterward? I mean, when the wings are gone the magic is gone, right?*

David goes to the window, looks out. It's a nice spring day with a sweet six-story drop. He thinks of Barn Bluff, the spring thermals, the *clicka-clicka* of bats, the fine, blown sand of mosquitoes on his skin, the glides and swoops. "You have a point."

*You'd have to ride the elevator down like everybody else.*

"Don't get smart or I'll put your head in a drawer."

*Seriously, what will you do without your wings? You'll be*

*just another guy on the street—more handsome, probably, but still just another guy.*

David doesn't answer; he stares out the window.

*Get in touch with some tabloid reporter. Market yourself. Go for the gold, the big time. Two shows nightly in Vegas. Take the money, surround yourself with chicks who don't care what you look like as long as you flash the green. I know I could get behind that.*

"Great life for about a week," David mutters.

*Or start a church. Saint Charles of the Ascension. Jesus did it once; you could do it every Sunday at nine and eleven.*

"*Ascension* means up, you idiot. I can only go down. There's sort of a difference."

*Up, down, big deal. People don't care which direction— they're just looking for some movement. Something they can latch on to, something they can believe in.*

David leans forward to look down at the lame, the halt, the wheelchair riders on the sidewalk below; he stares through his own bug-eyed reflection in the glass.

*I mean, you've already got a cult, man. Really, the more I think about it, let's keep the wings. With a face like mine and those fancy skin kites, we'd be bigger than Elvis.*

At that moment there is a discreet tap on the door. Cheetah pokes her head in. David makes a startled cry and rushes forward; they embrace, and he kisses her face all over. The Trotwoods stand shyly just behind her. Mrs. Trotwood is holding a padded brown mailing envelope.

"We heard voices," she says, glancing about the room. "We don't want to interrupt."

"We thought you were with a doctor or someone," Cheetah says; she, too, glances about the room.

"No, just me," David says. "And him." His first instinct was to hide New Guy—rip him off the wall, stash him under the mattress, stow him in the drawer with the Arabic magazines. But he doesn't, which feels like some kind of progress.

"And who's that?" Cheetah asks. They all look at New Guy.

"That would be me," David says.

There is silence. "I don't get it," Cheetah says.

"Me after my makeover."

Cheetah and the Trotwoods laugh.

David does not. Still holding hands with Cheetah, he steps closer to New Guy. Looks closely at his face.

"Seriously?" Cheetah says.

"Yes," David says without turning. "The surgeons mapped my face, then did that on their computer. That would be the new me."

"The surgeons could do that—and the . . . other operation, too?" Margaret asks.

David nods. "All at once. Soon, if I want."

They are all silent. Mrs. Trotwood, eyes fixed on New Guy, sets the envelope aside and sits down on the bed as if faint. As if it's all too much to take in.

Cheetah has turned very white. She looks pre-seizure.

"Why would you do that?" she says. "We're just getting used to you the way you are. *You're* just getting used to you the way you are!" She turns away from David and covers her face with her hands.

Earl Trotwood sits down as well. They look around the suite, but their eyes always come back to New Guy on the wall. David goes to Cheetah and holds her from behind. He looks over her head and out the window. The tops of the trees are well below; two robins flutter in their fine, green leaves. At street level a kid in a wheelchair, pushed by his parents, rolls along; his IV bag trembles from its skinny pole, and its clear fluid catches sunlight, which makes it glow.

"Maybe we should, I don't know, see a pastor or something," Margaret Trotwood says softly, as if talking to herself.

"Has anybody died here?" Earl replies.

"No," Margaret allows.

"But she's right—it might be like that," Cheetah blurts. "I mean, who David is now—that David would be gone."

They are silent. New Guy says nothing; he's shy around strangers. David turns to Mr. Trotwood. "They do make me see a shrink or somebody. I mean, before I'd have the surgery."

"Then you've made up your mind?" Cheetah asks.

David is silent.

"I think it's a good idea," Margaret says. She can't take her eyes off New Guy. "He certainly is a handsome young fellow."

Earl nudges her hard with his elbow. "Of course it's up to David," he says. "Whatever he decides, we're behind him one hundred percent."

"But do you want to *be* him?" Cheetah asks. She tears New Guy off the wall and thrusts him in David's face.

"I don't know. I don't know!" David says. He takes Cheetah by the chin—roughly—and forces her to look closely at his face. "Would you look this way if you didn't have to?"

She jerks away from him; his anger has frightened her. He turns, feeling the burn in his eyes, and stands before the window, where as usual, his bug-eyed ghost in the glass stares back at him.

"I . . . have to go," Cheetah says, and hurries out the door.

"Oh dear," Margaret Trotwood says. In the silence that follows, her gaze falls to the envelope. "There's mail for you, David," she says brightly. "We found this in our box this morning. I think it's get-well cards from your friends at school."

"Get well?" David says, his anger surging back. He ignores the envelope and stalks back to the window. "I'm supposed to 'get well'?"

Later that afternoon David meets again with Dr. Ramaswamy, this time not in a bedroom but at his office. The examination is more detailed, complete with blood and skin-tissue samples; there are long periods of waiting in

small rooms. In another wide, bright room, David under-
goes an MRI; lying on his back, his skull strapped down
tightly, he slowly passes through a humming tunnel, then
out the other side. Throughout the afternoon Dr. Ramaswamy seems slightly distracted—checks his watch
often—as he briskly comes and goes. Then David hears
voices beyond the door: the rising, melodic notes of the
doctor's voice as if he is greatly pleased. Soon the door
opens, and three doctors come in. Two are dressed in
slightly rumpled suits, as if they have been traveling a
long way. One has a gray beard; the other is clean-shaven
and carries a plastic bag that reads "New York, New
York."

"Charles!" the two men say at once.

"It's David now," Dr. Ramaswamy says quickly. "David,
may I introduce to you to my former colleagues, Doctors
Akbar and Wisman."

David reluctantly shakes their hands.

"How you've grown!" says Dr. Akbar.

"Remarkable," adds Dr. Wisman.

The three doctors gather around David and smile un-
ceasingly at him.

"Gentlemen?" says Dr. Ramaswamy.

"Oh, I almost forgot—we brought you something," says
Dr. Akbar to David.

"Some small gifts from home, as it were," adds Dr. Wisman.

David looks inside the sack. There is a souvenir replica

of the Statue of Liberty plus a bag of genuine New York bagels. He holds the bagels to his nose, then lifts the small green lady with upraised arm.

"Thank you," he begins, but his throat catches. He has to look away.

"Our pleasure," says Dr. Akbar.

"To be sure," says Dr. Wisman.

"I have asked my colleagues here to consult with me—on you, David—and assist me with the operation."

David turns to Dr. Ramaswamy. "I thought we're still deciding."

"Yes, of course. There I go again, way ahead of myself."

"From what Dr. Ramaswamy says, you're a perfect candidate," Dr. Wisman says.

"May we?" Dr. Akbar asks David. And this time all three doctors examine him from top to bottom. As they murmur back and forth, finishing one another's sentences, speaking in their specialized medical tongue, David gradually suspends himself in air. Leaves his body. Hovers somewhere near the ceiling. When he looks down, the boy on the table is skinny and pale and surrounded by doctors. His eyes are squeezed shut and he is not crying, but he is the ugliest freak David has ever seen. *Why go through life looking like that?* New Guy whispers. *You'd be crazy not to do it.*

Back in his room (the Trotwoods and Cheetah are checking in to a motel and will return), David flops onto his

king-size bed and flips on the television. Any channel will
do. His eyes go the envelope. After a while, he reaches for
it, tears it open. The return address reads "Oak Leaf," but
inside are no get-well cards. Just a DVD in a thin plastic
case. No note. No label.

David lies back on his bed and turns the DVD over and
over in his hands. His life is a bad television movie complete with an unmarked package; the arrival of unmarked
things—especially DVDs—is never a good sign. He considers tossing it on the floor and stomping it. Tossing its
shiny, sharp fragments into the trash. But he's only human.

He goes to the entertainment center, powers up, and
waits, heart beginning to *thrum-thrum* as the DVD loads.
Where movie titles should be, text rolls:

*David, dude, you're busted. Gotcha! We seen you fly off
Barn Bluff that night, and it took us a while to put two
and two together. We started to watch you at school, but
then when you ended up in the hospital and weirded out
everyone, we knew it had to be you. Lucky for me, my un-
cle's a janitor there, and he knows everything. He even told
me what room you were in, so I could stake out your window. So look at this video and then think about what you
want to do. All I know is that we could make big money,
David. I could sell this to CNN or somebody right now,
but Janet says we could make more money if we worked together. So think about what you want to do—but not too
long. Your friend, Max (and Janet).*

The screen flashes to a brick wall, then a window—the
Red Wing hospital—where a figure steps up to the glass.

David swears, forgets to breathe as he watches himself
slide clumsily through the narrow opening, then stand
upright on the sill. His arms raise, his skin kites swell, he
bounces on his toes three times (the toe thing he was un-
aware of)—then jumps. He sucks in a breath not so
much at the concrete coming up fast but at the sight of
his wings, which are way bigger than he imagined: wider,
fuller, more reaching, and prettier, too—the color of a
monarch's wings—against the brown brick wall. He
makes a running landing, churning his legs like a man on
a hang glider (he gives himself an eight out of ten score),
then gathers in his arms and their floppy skin and hustles
into the alley. The camera shakily probes the mouth of
the alley, then tracks back up the hospital wall to the window, where Cheetah stands like a silhouette David has
left behind. The video goes jerky and black.

*Now you're up against it,* New Guy whispers. *Now we
gotta clip the wings for sure.*

David replays the DVD, watches himself over and over
until he hears shuffling outside on the hallway carpet. It's
the Trotwoods and Cheetah. For long moments after they
tap on the door, he doesn't move; he stares at the ceiling
until they tap again, then finally gets up to let them in.
Mrs. Trotwood starts to say something cheerful, then goes
silent.

Earl Trotwood, too, senses something. "Are you all right, son?"

David motions for the Trotwoods to sit down. He is strangely calm, relaxed even. He sits between his parents, then points the remote at the big-screen television. "There's something I want you to see."

# 20

At dinner that night, an all-you-can-eat buffet, Mrs. Trotwood barely touches her food. She is alternately weepy and staring. This being Rochester, no one looks twice. Earl Trotwood eats for all of them, great, heaping plates of ribs and potatoes, but with faraway eyes—food helps him think, David has come to see.

"What do we do now?" Mrs. Trotwood murmurs to no one in particular.

"It will come to us," Earl Trotwood says. There's a bright sheen of sweat on his forehead.

"Us?" David says sharply—then is sorry.

"It's okay, son," Earl says. "You've got a lot on your mind."

Margaret covers David's hand with hers but won't meet his eyes.

David glances to Cheetah. She hasn't eaten a bite.

The next morning he meets with the shrink, Dr. Faricy,

a soft-spoken black woman with unblinking dark eyes. She is wearing bright African colors, and he expects her to have a strange accent, but she sounds more midwestern than Margaret Trotwood. "Hello, David," she says as they shake hands. "I'm here to make sure you're not crazy."

Dr. Faricy is witty and nice, but her eyes probe David's. He looks away.

"First we'll do some word and math-type questions," she says. "They might seem kind of stupid, but they tell me important things about your cognitive processes."

David is silent; he feels that familiar departure sensation—his brain leaving his body, his head detaching from his shoulders.

"I'm going to read some sequences, and I want you to repeat them back to me."

David listens as she describes a car driving east for six blocks, turning left, then continuing on for sixteen blocks, and so on. After a dozen turns, Dr. Faricy pauses. "Repeat, if you can, the path of our car. Do as many turns as you can recall."

David repeats them all, rapidly.

Dr. Faricy raises an eyebrow. "Very good. I should have such memory." She marks something on her chart, then rolls her chair closer to David. She lays out a photo of New Guy on the table. "So, David, let's talk . . ."

They do so for an hour, a chess game of a conversation,

in which David is careful not to lose territory, be cornered, forget who's who, lose his king. Whoever his king is nowadays.

"New Guy is New Guy; I'm still me," he says at one point.

"But could you become better acquainted? Even friends?" Dr. Faricy asks.

"We'd have to, wouldn't we?" David says with exasperation.

She glances at her watch. "I think we're about done here."

"Sorry," David says, "I didn't mean—"

"No, no—don't be sorry. I meant we're done here in a good way. I think you're one of the most well-adjusted patients I've seen in months. There's no reason why you can't have the surgery."

*You see, dude? Now what are you waiting for?*

The next day, David has free time while the doctors consult. New Guy won't shut up, so he walks the maze of the Mayo complex. Cheetah and the Trotwoods had to go home (they'll be back); he can reach them by phone, but their voices sound different—strange—or maybe he's imagining things.

Down in the underground is a great place to people-watch. The Mayo Clinic and related buildings are connected by a subterranean web of fluorescent-lit concourses where patients on gurneys and in wheelchairs or electric carts pass from one building, one exam, to the next. It's a parade of injuries and diseases that makes him feel better. At least he doesn't have brain cancer or some large part of him missing.

The underground also offers shopping for all manner of medical supplies. He pauses before a window display of walkers; spotlit is "Pro Walker," with titanium (not aluminum) legs plus the latest in gel handgrips. He moves on past crutches "For All Body Types, Including Plus-Size!" (the shafts are bowed outward for really fat people), then a store specializing in home oxygen supplies, including the "Kronos All-day Tank," built to look like a woman's oversize purse.

Suddenly a kid's voice behind him calls, "Hey! Hey, Weird Dude!"

David stiffens. For an instant he's back in Valley View High. But he turns around to see the wheelchair kid. From the Kahler Hotel elevator.

"It's me, Brandon," the kid says cheerfully. He face is not so puffy, but his color is burnt-corn yellow. His electric cart carries a pole and an IV bag. His parents are not with him.

"Hey, little dude," David says.

"What are you still doing here?" Brandon says. "I thought you said nothing was wrong with you."

"I'm back," David says. "I might be getting another makeover."

"With a better doctor this time?"

"We can only hope."

Brandon vibrates with laughter. "That's what I need, a makeover. Except I'd have to have, like, an everything makeover. A total body transplant."

David is silent.

"You like my chair?" Brandon touches a button and spins a 360.

"Neat," David says.

"It's faster than all the other termies'," Brandon says. "We have races."

"Termies?"

"Dead kids. Like me," Brandon says, and spins another 360.

"You don't look dead," David says.

"Check back in a month," Brandon says, and laughs wildly.

David glances around. "So where are your parents today?"

"At a POD group meeting."

"POD?"

"Parents of Dead Kids," Brandon says, and cracks up again.

"So, what, you're out cruising for chicks?" David says.

Brandon grins widely.

"Who knows?" David says. "With a cool ride like this, you might get lucky."

"I know where we can get free food," Brandon says suddenly. "Want to come?"

In a small cafeteria that even David doesn't know about, they eat. Actually, David eats, some nachos with pale melted cheese over the top, while Brandon sips a root beer long on ice, short on beer.

"I thought you were hungry," David says.

"I am. I'm eating as we speak." He jerks his head toward the IV bag, then closes his eyes and smacks his lips as if savoring the moment. "I think it's . . . chicken today. Actually, it's chicken every day."

"You're a funny kid, you know that?" David says.

"I could do stand-up comedy, right?"

"No, it'd have to be sit-down," David says.

Brandon gives him a clammy high five. "Let's do something," he says. "Go somewhere."

"Like where?"

"We could shoot some hoops," Brandon says. "Go skateboarding? Bust some moves on a half-pipe?"

"All right, all right," David says. "Enough of that."

"Sorry," Brandon says.

"We can at least hang out," David says.

"Okay," Brandon says immediately. "Let's play Good News / Bad News."

"Go ahead," David says cautiously.

"Bad news: I'm in this stupid Make-A-Wish program. You know what that is?"

"Sort of."

"It's this lame program where, because I'm dying—bone cancer, by the way—I get one wish to do anything I like."

"What's lame about having a wish come true?" David asks.

"Because kids are so predictable," Brandon says. "Most of them ask to, like, go to Disney World. Or swim with dolphins—that's the other big one. But this one kid from Montana really stuck it to them. His wish was to go on a big-game hunt in Alaska and shoot some kind of endangered bear—a grizzly, I think."

"I think I read about that," David says.

"It was cool!" Brandon says. "How could they say no?"

"So how about the good news part?" David asks.

Brandon leans forward: there is a surge of light, a flash of energy in his yellowish eyes. "I've got an even better wish. I've told hardly anyone. Just my parents and a couple of termies, but they're already dead."

"So what is it?" David asks. "Your wish."

"You know how parents make you go to church, Sunday school, confirmation, and all that stuff?"

"Yes," David says.

"Well, I went through all that. And here's my wish: I don't want to go anywhere, I don't want to do anything, I just want someone to prove to me that God really is up there."

They are silent.

"Brilliant, yes?" Brandon says, and spins a 360.

"Supreme," David says.

"I knew you'd like it!" Brandon says, and spins his chair yet again. "I knew it!"

"It's so far beyond swimming with the dolphins or shooting a bear."

"Exactly!" Brandon says. He lets out a long laugh, then slumps in his chair; it's as if his batteries—his own—have suddenly run down.

"Are you all right?" David asks quickly.

"I should get back," Brandon says.

"Where?"

"Children's."

"Children's? That's blocks away."

Brandon shrugs. "It's usually pretty dead over there—if you know what I mean—so I catch a shuttle over here to Mayo." He manages a giggle.

"I'll take you back, little dude."

"Thanks," Brandon murmurs, and slumps lower. "Don't worry if I doze off along the way."

David quickly gets Brandon's cart moving toward the elevator. They catch a shuttle (Brandon falls fully asleep on the way) and ride west to Children's. Brandon wakes up as his cart jolts off the ramp and onto the sidewalk. "Straight through those doors," he says. The Children's lobby has the usual bank of empty wheelchairs, along with bright red custom pedal cars for kids. The pedals are gone, and the poles for IV bags double as pushing handles for nurses or parents.

"Second floor, teen lounge," Brandon says. His eyes are yellower and his voice thinner.

David quickly punches the elevator number (he sees himself in the brushed chrome mirror but thinks nothing of it). The door opens on a lobby center and two bronze statues of children. The life-size bronze children, seated, look down into a courtyard where colorful tulips (real ones) are blooming. Beyond the lobby the hospital hallway is brightly decorated and busy.

"In a month, that's me," Brandon says, tilting his head toward the nearest statue.

"They are a little creepy," David says.

A nurse spots them and hurries forward. "There you are, Brandon, you rascal!" he says. "Your parents are worried sick."

"Not this sick I hope."

The nurse groans but gives Brandon a brief high five; he nods to David. "Thanks."

"No problem," David says. He is about to leave when Brandon's parents rush around the corner.

"Brandon, you drive us crazy when you take off like that!" the mother says.

"Sorry," Brandon says. "I was just hanging with David."

The parents look at David.

"The elevator? Kahler Hotel," David says.

"Of course," the father says. "Hello again. Thanks for rescuing Brandon." He has several days of whiskers and looks as if he has been sleeping in his clothes. The mother has very tired eyes.

"It wasn't really a rescue," David says. "We ran into each other down in the underground at Mayo."

"Mayo?" the mother says with alarm. "You were all the way over there?"

"Sorry," Brandon says, with a wink at David.

"Let's get you into bed for a while," the nurse says, and steers Brandon forward.

"David, thanks again," the father says.

"No problem. He's a great kid."

The mother smiles wanly. There is a moment of dead airtime. "Do you want to look around?" she asks. "See how we live?"

"Or don't," Brandon calls over his shoulder; he laughs at his own joke as he disappears into his room.

"I'm sorry," the mother says.

"It's okay," David says. "I'm getting used to it."

They take the tour, pausing along a brightly decorated wall of small squares. "Every child paints a ceramic tile," the mother explains, pausing to touch one with a sun, a beach, and seagulls. "They're added to the wall."

"Brandon won't do one, of course," the father adds; there is a measure of pride in his voice.

"And just ahead, the teen lounge," the mother says.

David looks inside. It's decorated with pink and purple, including a large booth for hanging out, plus all manner of board and older electronic games. It's also empty.

"Brandon used to spend quite a bit of time in here," the mother says, "but lately he won't have anything to do with this place. Every chance he gets, he takes off."

"He seems to know his way around," David offers.

"As do we all," the father says.

They keep walking. They pass more parents—the healthy ones—pushing pale children in wheelchairs or holding their arms as they totter along. Many of the kids have no hair, or faces the color of concrete.

"How long has Brandon been here?" David asks.

"About eight months."

"Where do you live? I mean your real home," David adds.

"I don't know anymore," the father says; he looks out the window.

"North Dakota," the mother says quickly. "A small town called Grafton."

"Do you go home? Like on weekends?"

"Not without Brandon," the father says.

"Brandon doesn't travel well these days," the mother adds. "Hasn't for a couple of months now."

The father looks around. "All of this becomes your life." He gestures at the hallways, the lounge. "It's like you've always lived here. Your old life is something you maybe read once, or saw in a television movie. But this is reality. This is where you live and always will live."

His wife takes his arm.

He blinks. "Sorry, honey," he says.

"That's okay, dear," she says, and touches his face. His whiskers. "You should shave tonight. In fact, I'll shave you. Would you like that?"

"You don't have to shave me."

"I'll do it. I want to," the mother says.

"Listen, I should probably get back," David says.

The mother blinks, as if remembering he's beside them. "Of course. I'm sorry. We didn't mean to keep you."

"You haven't. I enjoyed meeting Brandon again."

"We'll walk you out," the father says.

In the lobby, beside the staring bronze children, they shake hands.

"Did he tell you about his Make-A-Wish?" the mother says.

David nods.

The couple manage smiles of exactly the same weight: wry and small. "Somehow I thought he might have," the mother adds.

"It's . . . pretty unique," David says.

"Any advice?" the father says. "We're open."

David shrugs. He looks out the window and points to

the garden below. "I dunno. Maybe the tulips? Spring?" He scratches his head.

"Tried all that," the mother says, her eyes sad but with a tiny sparkle of laughter. "Brandon says he wants something bigger. 'Something more obvious.'"

"Don't we all," says the father.

# 21

David is barely in the elevator when New Guy starts talking. *Hey, at least you've got a choice. That poor kid is screwed.*

"Shut up," David replies. But New Guy keeps at it—talking incessantly—so David, once outside, walks faster. Heading back toward Mayo, he moves rapidly along the street, weaving among the limpers and the wheelchair bound. *Look at that dude,* New Guy says, *that male nurse—isn't he a handsome devil? You could look like him.* "Yeah, right," David says, and walks faster still, walking anywhere a light turns green, a door opens. Then he catches sight of himself, reflected in glass windows, stalking along in full conversation—gesturing, arguing, muttering.

He pulls up. Shuts up. Glancing over his shoulder, he sees only some nurses receding down the climate-controlled pedestrian skyway. How he got up here, he is

not sure. Outside, the sun is shining, and he takes the
first exit down to street level and fresh air.

He's heading east on Third Street away from the Mayo
complex. *Hey, where we going?* New Guy asks with
some alarm. David says, "I'll let you know when we get
there." The farther David walks from the medical complex, the fainter New Guy's voice; like an Internet wire-
less hot spot, he seems to have limited range, which
cheers David considerably. Ahead is a movie theater and
retail complex complete with a large bookstore—inside
of which New Guy goes dead. Clearly he's not into
books.

David wanders the shelves, looking more at the people—normal, undiseased, uninjured people—than at the
books. A young couple, high school age, are having a coffee date. A short, athletic-looking, blond-haired guy, not
fully at home in a bookstore, is sitting at a little round
table with an attractive, slightly alternative-looking girl
(hoop earrings, a touch of Goth in her eye shadow). She's
not a real Goth, and he's not an athlete-as-cliché. They
have things in common. They like each other a lot. She
leans forward and touches his arm; he looks down at her
hand and traces his pointer finger on a vein, following it
across the back of her hand and up her wrist. She laughs
and pulls away her hand; they both take drinks of their
tall coffees, then sit grinning at each other. No deformities. No baggage. No issues.

Suddenly the girl turns to David—she feels his gaze.

Her eyes widen, and she leans forward and whispers urgently to her date. David ducks out of sight, hurries along the shelves, then down the escalator and out of the store.

At street level his shoulders slump, and he heads back to Mayo. "Okay, okay!" he says tiredly to New Guy.

Back in his suite, David calls Dr. Ramaswamy—has him paged—then afterward, he dials the Trotwoods' number. Earl picks up the phone. "I'm going to have the operations," he blurts. "I've talked to Dr. Ramaswamy."

"When?" Earl Trotwood asks. There is clattering, then David hears Margaret breathing into the receiver.

"In three days. That's the soonest they could schedule me."

Mr. Trotwood is silent.

"I'm sure it's for the best," Margaret says, relief in her voice.

"It's your decision," Mr. Trotwood says after a pause.

When David calls Cheetah and tells her, she bursts into tears. It's as if she's dragging her cell phone across sandpaper. "I'm coming to Rochester. Tomorrow morning, early. Don't do anything until I get there."

"Ah, okay," he says, somewhat surprised. At least he'll have some company for the day.

*She worries me,* New Guy says. *Girls will throw you off your game. Then again, remember that chick Tara from Valley View? The track star with the long legs? Once we get through the surgery, you should call her up.*

David switches off the lights and covers his ears with pillows.

In the morning, at breakfast in the Mayo cafeteria, Cheetah can't stop crying. So David talks. Makes conversation. "Hey, remember that kid, Brandon?" he says. "I ran into him again." He tells her about Brandon's supreme Make-A-Wish.

"Let's go see him," Cheetah says, snuffling, looking around. "I hate this cafeteria."

# 22

Brandon, propped up in bed, is smaller and his eyes darker yellow. "Mom, Dad—visitors!"

The father jerks in the chair he is dozing in; the mother sits up on the trundle bed below the window and fluffs her hair.

"Sorry, didn't mean to wake you," David says.

"No, that's fine. We had sort of a bad night," the mother says, and musters a smile.

"Mind if we hang out with Brandon for a while?" Cheetah asks.

"Of course not—no," the parents say as one.

"You could go get some coffee or something," Brandon says to them.

"You're sure?" the dad says. He looks to his wife.

"It's not like I'm going anywhere," Brandon says.

"Yeah, we've heard that before," the dad replies. They pause in the doorway as if they can't step through.

"We'll stay right here until you get back," David says. And then they are alone with Brandon.

He turns to Cheetah. "I was thinking: do you have any girlfriends? Ones that might like to hook up with a nearly dead kid?"

"I do know this Goth chick, but she likes completely dead boys."

"Ha ha" is all Brandon can say. But he smiles.

"David told me about your Make-A-Wish," Cheetah says.

Brandon grins. "Cool, huh?"

"Very," Cheetah says.

"It's actually for my parents. They're having a pretty hard time, and I kinda worry about them afterward."

David and Cheetah glance at each other.

"My dad especially," Brandon says. "I worry that he might crack up or something. Or they'll get divorced. That happens a lot, I read."

David gets a giant lump in his throat.

Cheetah swallows. "What would it take? For your Make-A-Wish to come true?"

Brandon's eyes go to the window. "Something really big. Really amazing."

Cheetah turns to David. *Oh no—not that,* New Guy says.

"What if your wish came true?" she asks, eyes still on David.

Brandon looks at her. "Fat chance."

"You could be wrong."

Brandon shuts his eyes. "I seriously doubt it."

"Excuse me, could I talk with you?" David says to Cheetah. He grabs her arm and pulls her out of the room. "What are you doing?"

"It just came to me," she says, light flashing in her eyes. "Something you could do for Brandon—especially since you're going to have the operation."

David glares at her. "What?"

"You know very well what," Cheetah says.

He turns away.

"I mean, hey, it's not a lot to ask, considering," she says.

David could not be more annoyed.

She comes up and hugs him from behind. Hugs him until his iceberg melts. "One last time," she says. "Think of it that way."

They go back into Brandon's room.

"Okay, little dude," David says. "I'm your guy."

Brandon stares, then musters a laugh that ends raspy and small. "You? You prove that God is up there? Wouldn't it be more, like, the reverse?"

David is annoyed with both of them but goes ahead and says it. "The thing of it is, little dude—I'm sort of like an angel."

Brandon's eyes close from silent laughter. Tears run down his cheeks.

"I have wings," David adds.

"Sure you do," Brandon says.

"Want to see them?" David says.

"Sure," Brandon says, "give it your best shot."

David glances at the door; Cheetah goes to it, peeks out, then closes it and props a chair against the latch. "Here goes," David says. He stands up, takes his shirt off, raises his arms, concentrates.

Brandon's eyes bug wide. He jerks upright in bed. His mouth hangs open.

"See? You didn't believe me," David says.

"Jeez!" Brandon whispers. "Who are you? Some kind of ugly angel?"

"Great," David mutters to Cheetah as he tucks in his bundled-up shirt.

"Hey, nobody said angels have to be blond and beautiful," Cheetah answers.

"But they do have to fly," Brandon says. His eyes gleam.

David looks to Cheetah.

"He can fly," Cheetah says, "but he needs way more space than this room." She motions David toward the window. They look out. David surveys the building, the rooftops opposite; he shrugs.

"Are you sure?" Cheetah says to David.

He nods.

"When?" Brandon says to them. "It's gotta be soon."

David and Cheetah turn to look at Brandon. Cheetah tugs David to the side of the room, where they confer.

"How about tomorrow morning, real early?" David says to Brandon.

"I'm there," Brandon says. "I'll have a nurse wheel my bed into the lobby."

"The lobby? Can't you see it from here?"

"Naw, the window's too small. The view is way better from the lobby."

David looks at Cheetah with concern.

"I'll tell her I want to be alone to look at the tulips," Brandon adds, managing a dry laugh.

"All right," David says. "But you can't tell anyone, not even your parents. This is just for you. We need to keep this on the down-low."

"Got it," Brandon says.

"Tomorrow morning, seven o'clock, before there's any-body around," David says again.

"I'm there, I'm there, I'm there!" Brandon chants. "Oh, man, I can't believe it." He is suddenly full of energy—as if he has been plugged into a battery charger. And at that moment his parents return. They, too, have better color, as if they have had a transfusion of some kind—or at least strong coffee.

"Well, we gotta go," David says quickly.

"Thanks," Brandon's parents say. The mother gives them each a quick hug.

"See you tomorrow," Brandon calls, then laughs like a maniac at their little secret.

In the morning, David and Cheetah meet up early. The sun is barely up as they slip into Mary Brigh Courtyard.

The tulip blossoms are still closed. David looks around one more time to make sure there are no obstructions, no wires, no problems. He shades his eyes and looks up toward the children's hospital. The windows of the second-floor lobby are empty.

"I hope he comes soon," Cheetah whispers.

After a last look about, they head inside the hospital building opposite and up the elevator. They are careful to look behind them, watch their backs—but no one follows. Pretending to examine some artwork in the lobby, they waste a few minutes until the coast is clear, then duck into the stairwell. At the top floor there is some fumbling with the emergency exit latch (which David has cased ahead of time). And it opens to the roof.

"Please, be careful!" Cheetah says.

"Yes, dear," he says sarcastically and gives her a kiss.

"I'll wait for you by the tulip garden."

He nods, then steps onto the roof as the door quietly latches behind him.

Pigeons rattle up—David flinches as they flutter away. They have been sitting where the sun first strikes. He keeps a low profile along the humming air conditioners and giant fans. *What do you think is in hospital exhaust?* New Guy asks.

"I don't know," David mutters.

*And you don't want to know.* New Guy laughs.

Keeping low, David draws near the edge. After a glance at his watch, he waits another minute, then carefully eases his head above the short, asphalt lip of the roof. Shading his eyes, he squints down. Cheetah waves from a shadowy far corner past the tulips. He waves back. She continues to wave. Point actually. Pointing urgently toward the children's lobby windows.

"Oh no!" David says. *You see? I told you this is stupid,* New Guy taunts. The windows are filled with people. David ducks down, then cautiously looks again. Not people, kids. Pale kids in paler hospital gowns. Some lean on walkers. Some slump in wheelchairs. Others, like Brandon, are propped upright in beds near kids who have pushed them. At least twenty kids there, and not a sign of an adult. It's Brandon's supreme hospital insurrection.

"Here we go," David says to New Guy. New Guy doesn't answer; he's scared witless.

David stands up suddenly. In the children's lobby windows there is movement; the kids crowd closer, touch their hands to the glass. David strips off his shirt, lets it flutter to the ground, counting "One thousand one, one thousand two . . ." There is plenty of space and height — no reason he can't do this. He steps up onto the lip, closes his eyes. Concentrates. Spreads his wings. The sun catches them; he can feel its warmth in his skin, in its thin, tough pinkness; blood flows through the spidery veins.

It is his most graceful launch ever. Like an Acapulco cliff diver, he arches forward and catches the air exactly right. The sun is striking fully on him at that moment, and he busts a nice—but careful—bank to the right, then the left. He is able to pass close by the windows, even wave. He sees the children's mouths hang open and their faces fill with awe. Brandon has raised his arms in victory, as if he, too, is flying.

David touches down clumsily in the flower bed but doesn't embarrass himself by pitching over and eating tulips. Cheetah hurries forward with his shirt, which he pulls on.

*That's it?* New Guy says. *That's our Grand Finale?*

"Let's go!" David says urgently.

"Wait, David. Look!" Cheetah says.

He turns. In the windows the kids are clapping. Their mouths are open, and their hands hit together again and again without sound.

# 23

Afterward, hiding out in a nearby park, David is silent.

"What's wrong?" Cheetah asks.

"Nothing's wrong."

"Sure it is."

David toys with his souvenir tulip, still closed. "I shouldn't have done it."

*I agree,* New Guy says.

Cheetah touches his hand. "It was beautiful. Seeing those kids there clapping, I mean, God."

*See what I mean?* New Guy says. *First you're an angel, now you're God. Keep going this way, and you'll never get those wings clipped.*

They continue sitting in the sunshine in silence.

*Cheetah's a nice girl, but think of the chicks you could have if you looked like me. Think of it, man. Remember that blonde, Shannon Olson, from Valley View? How hot she was? She's yours. All of her. And her friend*

*Alison? The brunette volleyball player? Those girls would fight over you, dude—assuming you had my chin, of course.*

"What?" Cheetah asks.

"Nothing."

"I swear you said something."

"Just thinking aloud."

"Thinking what?"

"That I should go back and tell Brandon the truth."

"What truth?"

Everybody is silent, even New Guy.

"That I'm no angel," David says. There is sudden anger in his voice.

"Why would you want to do that?"

"Because!" David says, louder. For a moment that's the only word he can think of. "Because it's cruel otherwise. It's a trick, it's . . ."

"Please," Cheetah says, clutching his wrist. "At least give Brandon a day to believe in what he saw. What's the harm in that?"

He pulls away from her. "All right. A day. But I'm having the operation. Nothing you can do will make me change my mind."

Cheetah looks bewildered. "I should go," she says abruptly. "I'll come back tomorrow for your operation. At least I think I will." Her voice catches, and she hurries away, toward the parking ramp.

•   •   •

In the morning, his last day as a freak, David gets up early and heads over to Children's. On the way he rehearses his lines—what he'll say to Brandon—but is distracted by how nice a morning it is. The sun is still low; the humid air has warmth, body, fragrance. He thinks of Barn Bluff, the great thermals certain to be rising at sundown.

*Yeah, well, you know what happened the last time you dove off there,* New Guy says.

"My fault entirely. No way that would happen again."

*Not after today, it won't,* New Guy says.

He checks his watch: six hours until he's under the knife. Something flutters and skitters in his stomach. He puts his head down and focuses on Brandon. "Hey, little dude, I gotta be honest," he practices. "What you saw . . ."

*Was more freak than angel. Somebody who should be in a sideshow. You want to see an angel? Ring your nurse. Now, those people are angels, and they're the only ones around.*

"Shut up!" David says loudly. An old lady out inspecting her flowers looks at him, then retreats onto her porch.

At the hospital he takes a deep breath, then slides into the elevator. On the second floor the elevator door opens to the two bronze kids—and a whole bunch of real ones. They are hanging around the lobby, some looking out through the glass as if waiting for something. Brandon's parents are talking animatedly—he hears them well before he sees them. They both sound energized—and happy. It's as if there has been a miracle cure, as if they and Brandon are going home.

Then David rounds the corner and sees the cluster of reporters, the outstretched microphones, the bright camera lights. He swears to himself, and ducks away, taking the long way to Brandon's room.

Which is silent.

Empty but for the bed.

The bed stripped down to the plastic-covered mattress. It shines in the spring sunlight. The bed and a small box of Brandon's things parked by the door.

"Oh no," David whispers. He sits down on the empty bed.

"Can I help you?" a voice says. It's a nurse, of course; she pauses in the doorway.

"Brandon?" David says. He touches the bed, the plastic sheet, but can't say anything else.

"I'm so sorry. His parents are in the lobby. You should speak with them."

"No, that's all right!" David says.

"Really," the nurse says. "I remember you visiting here. You were a friend of Brandon's. They'd want to see you."

The nurse takes his arm, so David is trapped once again. In the lobby, Brandon's mother calls out David's name, then pulls him into her arms. Reporters turn his way. The father hugs him awkwardly as well; he has shaved, and there are tiny razor nicks on his neck.

"He's gone, David," the mother says. "Last night."

David can't think of any words. Not one.

"But it happened!" the father says hoarsely. "It came true."

"His wish," the mother says urgently, holding on to David's arm. She looks around, lowers her voice. "The one he told you?"

David glances sideways, toward the door, but he is cornered.

"Look at this," the father says. He thrusts a small square ceramic tile into David's hands. The reporters jostle one another to get the close-up shot. The tile is painted, shakily and crudely: tall building, a stick figure with wings gliding toward black tulips. A very ugly angel. The drawing is signed Brandon.

"Something happened here yesterday," the father says, turning to the press, his voice cracking and triumphant. "The other kids saw it, too. Look at them. None of them will talk about it, but it has to be true!" His hand shakes as he holds up Brandon's tile.

The nurse puts her hand on his shoulder and steers him away from the reporters. "On this floor we see many things," she says softly, "things we don't talk about, things beyond words."

Brandon's father weeps for real now. His wife holds him. Cameras roll.

"That's all," the nurse says, shielding Brandon's parents from the lights. "Please, have some respect."

David seizes the moment to ooze away, through the

lobby and past the kids left behind. Some sit facing the window, the sun full on their pale faces; others are drawing or coloring—angels, of course. A kid in a wheelchair is molding a flying figure in damp, brown clay. He leans forward, fully focused, tongue clamped between small white teeth, as he works on the wings. David waits, shoulders hunched, in front of the elevators, then ducks into one. He is almost in the clear—the door is a hand's width from closing—when a cameraman blocks it with his foot. Several reporters and media people crowd in with him. Speaking into cell phones or scribbling notes, they don't give David a second glance. "It's that 'injured angel,' " a blond woman with stiff hair and lots of makeup says into her cell phone. "He's here somewhere!"

# 24

By noon, the news is fully out. All the local television stations run their Children's Hospital angel-sighting story. CBS ups the ante, with Katie Couric arriving for a live broadcast from the Mary Brigh Courtyard. "It's my understanding that CBS is close to obtaining actual footage of this so-called injured angel in flight," she says, wide-eyed and intense. "Stay with your CBS affiliates for a first look at what could only be called a miracle. We hope to bring you that footage on our evening news broadcast—if not before."

"Max," David says. "He's been busy."

Cheetah points the remote at the television.

"No—leave it on," David says. "I might as well get my fifteen minutes of fame." His laugh rings hollow in the suite, where he, Cheetah, and the Trotwoods are holed up. The wall clock reads 12:04; he has to check in at 1:00 p.m. for the presurgery routines. His stomach growls—no food allowed before an operation—and he takes another sip of ice water.

"It's too late for those pesky reporters," Mrs. Trotwood says suddenly. "By the end of the day there won't be a story—they'll all look like fools!"

David is surprised by the anger in her voice. Mr. Trotwood paces the floor; this is all too much for him, and David worries that he might have a heart attack, a stroke.

"I need to get out of here," David says suddenly. "Some fresh air. Just for a few minutes."

"Shall we come with you?" Mrs. Trotwood says quickly.

"No. You wait here and try to relax," David says. He comes close and touches her shoulder.

She squeezes his hand and looks up into his face. "Just think, David," she begins, "in a few hours—"

"Gotta go," he says quickly, and jerks his chin at Cheetah.

Outside, in the hallway, New Guy starts up, but David won't listen, not when he's holding Cheetah. The smell of patchouli oil in her hair, the compactness of her body against his—it's enough to hold the whole world at bay.

"Let's go downstairs," she breathes. "Street level, and just sit for a few minutes."

They end up on the steps of a church, Calvary Episcopal, just down and across the street from the Mayo Clinic. From here they can spy on the gathering queue of television trucks prickly with antennas, with satellite

dishes erected on their roofs. Reporters mill around like a
school of minnows, ready to surge left or right, depending
upon where the big fish appears.

"Which would be me," David says to New Guy.

"Pardon?" Cheetah says.

"Sorry. Just thinking aloud," David says. New Guy murmurs something smart-mouth in return, but his voice is
faint—as if he has shrunken or receded—and David can't
make out his words. Why, David is not sure, but he'll take
it. He checks his watch. A bit more than an hour to go
before check-in. Under the Mayo marquee, reporters
surge toward a man in a black suit—a clinic spokesper-
son, David guesses. The man speaks for no more than ten
seconds, then leaves. The reporters fall back with disappointment, though they go nowhere.

At that moment, David turns to see a family coming
down the sidewalk. Two parents and a girl about thirteen
stretched out in a motorized wheelchair. A serious wheelchair, like a black-padded chaise longue, with straps that
hold her down. They come closer. The girl has blond
hair, bent limbs, and she drools, but her eyes are clear.
Her mother walks beside her, hand on the toggle switch,
steering the girl toward the church. "If an angel appears,
that means Jesus has spoken," the mother is saying.

"That's right," the tidy father in a short-sleeved white
shirt says. "Now it's our job to praise him."

The girl moans, a kind of angry growl; David gets the
feeling there's nothing wrong with her brain. She just

can't say things. At this particular moment she does not want to go to church—not that she's against going to church, but because she's thirteen. This is a good old-fashioned family squabble. As the family heads up the ramp toward the wide doors of the church, the girl starts to flail and kick her legs and grab at the toggle switch. She manages to turn her chair so it crashes sideways against the doorframe and won't go in.

"Okay, okay!" the mother says. "We'll go somewhere else."

The girl slumps back in the chair and lets out a softer moan. The family reverses direction and heads down the ramp and then around the corner.

"Cool kid," Cheetah says.

"For sure," David replies. They watch the family go out of sight.

David turns back to stare at the Mayo Clinic, at the throngs of people below, the soaring glass tower above. Which is when it hits him. They—the patients, the reporters, even the doctors—are all just people trying to be well, get well, stay alive. There is not that much difference between any of them, no matter who they are or what they look like. The girl who just passed—if he were thirteen, he could see making friends with her. Moans are not that hard to figure out. And then there are all those neat kids like Brandon.

He looks at Cheetah; she doesn't realize he's watching

her. She's toying with a blade of grass, content just to sit there beside him on these sharp-edged granite steps.

"What if I didn't?" he says to her.

She looks up quickly. "Didn't?"

"Have the operations."

She looks back to her single blade of grass, then up to the media trucks. "What about them?"

"I'll give the reporters what they want. Then maybe they'll go away."

"You'd do that?" Cheetah says, clutching his arm. "You wouldn't be afraid?"

David swallows. He's as scared as the day Jo-Jo and T-Boy cornered him on the fire escape. "Not if you help me," he whispers.

She hugs him harder than he believed possible.

They split up, Cheetah heading to the media trucks, David staying mostly out of sight across the street. He watches her, small among the crowd, tap a cameraman on the shoulder; he seems annoyed at first, then stiffens as he listens. When he turns suddenly to call to his crew, Cheetah slips away.

"Perfect," David breathes.

They meet back at the suite. Mr. and Mrs. Trotwood accept this change of plans very differently. "That's my boy!" Earl shouts, and hoists David off the ground.

"Easy, Pops!" David says.

Margaret cries—immediately and loudly—but gradually quiets as David hugs her. "But what will you—what will we—do now?" she asks.

"We'll figure that out, dear," Earl says. "It will come to us."

David gets on the phone to the surgical desk and Dr. Ramaswamy.

"Please, we must talk about this!" the doctor says.

"All right, but I've made up my mind," David says.

In the meantime, on the suite's entertainment center, Cheetah is burning copies of Max's DVD. "How many?" she asks.

"As many as you can," David replies.

Within twenty minutes, Dr. Ramaswamy and the other two doctors arrive. David is momentarily weak-kneed as they enter the room—it's the power of doctors—but this is also why he asked them to come here. Had he gone to the hospital, into their space, he might have wavered.

"Are you sure?" the two New York doctors say almost as one, and begin to press David for his reasons. Dr. Ramaswamy is quieter and mainly listens.

"Our first rule as doctors is to do no harm," he says at length.

They all turn to him.

"Maybe if we operate we would be harming."

Dr. Akbar replies, "We would not be harming, we'd be improving David!"

"I don't mean harming David, I mean harming something larger. Some part of God's, or at least nature's, plan."

"What was God's plan for David?" Margaret says quickly, almost angrily. "That's what I want to know."

"If he has the operation, we never *will* know," Earl says.

The physicians all turn to Earl. Earl the hog farmer.

"Exactly," Dr. Ramaswamy says, and laughs.

The other doctors grumble with disappointment, but Dr. Ramaswamy is cheerful. "We will stand with you, David. All of us together."

When Cheetah has burned the DVDs—one for each of the major networks—it's time. They take secret back corridors to the Mayo Clinic, emerging in the lobby and great hall. They can hear, beyond the glass foyer, the din of the crowd (David presses his earplugs tighter), see reporters jostling for the best position. As he approaches the wide front doors, television camera lights flare on. David flinches—Cheetah takes one of his hands, Dr. Ramaswamy the other—then he sees a small space roped off for kids in wheelchairs. A half dozen kids, pale but expectant, lean forward to look.

David feels Earl and Margaret tight behind him, feels their hands on his shoulders.

"Ready, son?" Earl says.

David swallows, nods. Keeping his eyes on the children, he steps forward through the door.